PRINCESS FOR THE SPACE COWBOY

MATCH MADE IN SPACE

PHOEBE BELLE

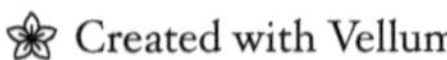 Created with Vellum

Hey, readers! This story spun to life in my brain and just wouldn't quit. What happens when an alien space cowboy who happens to be a prince needs a princess and his planet is short on women? Royalty is big in the tabloids on Earth, but that's about it. I started with this question and ran with it.

It starts on Earth and ends in space. In this world, we've already discovered life beyond Earth. There's space travel and other planets and all kinds of intergalactic fun stuff. There are other kinds of aliens, but we're starting with the space cowboys. They're smokin' hot, sexy, and kind of like Earth cowboys, except a little bigger, a little hotter, and super protective with gooey hearts of gold. They **worship** *women. On this planet, they need mates. Even better, they also need someone to find them.*

Chapter One

JANE

"Oooh! I can do that!"

I scroll on my phone screen, eyeing the job description.

Princess wanted for space cowboy in need of a wife. Additional job duties include recruiting other candidates for a matchmaking service on Aphroditea. Due to travel and relocation needs, preferred applicants must be able to move to a new planet. Requirement of no children or family at time of hire.

"Hmm. This has to be a joke, but what the hell? Might be fun to see what happens. I definitely don't have any kids."

I'm talking to myself. I'm also seriously tipsy.

You'd be tipsy too if you had my day.

"Hee, hee." I giggle to myself as I scroll through what has to be the biggest joke of a job advertisement I've ever seen.

"What do I have to lose?" I muse. I reach out with my free hand to reflexively pet my cat.

The second my hand lands on my comforter, I almost burst into tears. That's the thing. My cat died.

Creamsicle has been with me since I was ten years old. Since I'm now at the ripe old age of twenty-five, that meant he'd been with me for more than half of my life.

He died in his sleep. My vet said he probably died of heart failure.

"It comes in threes, right?" I murmur to myself.

My ex-fiancé screwed around on me. I found out the next day when I'd gone over to visit my best friend and found them tangled up in bed. Spoiler alert: they weren't just changing the sheets.

I'm counting that as two bad things because I lost my ex and my now-ex-best friend at once. Those two losses didn't hurt as bad as losing Creamsicle. Creamsicle had been all I had left of my family.

Pets count as family. I'm one of those people. If you feel like mocking me for it, then screw off. We definitely can't be friends.

Two years ago, my dad was found dead at his desk at work on the floor in his small hardware store that he'd loved so much. They said he had a massive heart attack. My mom died when she had me. Life had been me, my dad, and eventually Creamsicle, our unit against the world. I knew what it was like to be loved. But it seemed like I was out of luck lately.

So this ad? Some space cowboy needs a princess—what the hell? They also need someone who doesn't have any attachments on Earth. I'm free with no kids, no family, and no friends.

"Sign me up!" I exclaim as I tap the button to apply.

I scroll through, entering all the things they need. They even ask about my social media handles. They say it a little weird, though, calling it your *news handles*. I file that detail away in my brain.

All things considered, the application is pretty

simple. The big deal is I have to confirm I'm totally cool with going to space.

"Of course I'm cool with that," I say as my fingertips tap away on my phone screen.

I figure this whole thing is a big fat joke, but I've had a few glasses of wine and don't have anyone to talk to.

An hour or so later, I drowse into sleep, forgetting about my tipsy job application.

———

I wake up, rolling out of bed and plodding into the bathroom. I study myself in the mirror. My curly brown hair is a rumpled mess. "I excel at bedhead," I announce to myself in the mirror.

"I think I had a few too many glasses of wine last night," I add as I step into the shower.

This is what my life has become—me talking to myself. I don't remember applying for a job until I'm seated at my desk and my phone pings a few hours later.

I can't help it. I know better. *I really know better.* Doom-scrolling through GalaxyCosmo won't help me. Not at all. But I do it anyway. I keep wondering when freaking Kyle and Kylie will make it official online. Yeah, that's right. My ex's name is Kyle, and my ex-best friend's name is Kylie. I used to think it was cute that their names matched and meant something about me. But now they're together, and I'm alone. I'm pretty sure I missed all the signs until they hit me in the face.

My finger hovers over the screen. Because I want to know when they're going to have the nerve to post something about their newfound fuck buddy status or relationship. Kylie had left me this long, tearful message about how they fell in love. They couldn't help it, and it was meant to be, and blah, blah, blah, blah, blah.

Part of me wants them to post about it. I can't wait for them to get bashed to bits in the comments.

Whatever. I tap that notification and pull up the app.

"Huh?"

I speak loud enough that my cubicle mate, the one on the other side of that thin cardboard-and-fabric wall, calls over, "What?"

That's Stan. He's annoying and nosy.

"Oh, nothing," I say quickly.

I'm shocked to see I have a message.

We think you might be a great fit for us. Please come to our offices at 7 Space Rodeo Avenue, seventh floor.

I'm legit confused, but I bite my tongue just in time before I say anything else and prompt more nosiness from Stan.

I tap the main web browser on my phone to see just what I did on my phone last night. A job ad pops right up. I read it.

Oh no. Oh no, no, no, no. Oh fuck! What have I gone and done? I stand quickly, striding out of the doorway, if you can fucking call it that, of my cubicle and down the hallway. Blessedly, our cheap office has a bathroom where I can lock the door.

I check the time on my phone. It's five minutes from my lunch break. I abruptly decide I'm going to scout this place out.

I can't help but giggle as I reread the job description. Sober, with my headache barely at bay, I can't help but think even now this has got to be a joke. But what if it's not?

I've always wanted to leave Earth. Some people love our planet and wax poetic about how special it is. I'm sure it's pretty cool in the big scheme of things, but it's hot as hell, dry, and we've kind of screwed ourselves with the taking care of things. The past couple of weeks for me have been a shit show of epic proportions. I feel like life has wronged me.

I'm barely making ends meet. Ever since we made it to space, oh, like a few decades ago, I imagine it's like it used to be when cars first came around. Or maybe plane travel is a better example. Being able to go to space is a luxury very few can afford. You need to have job skills where they want to send you up there, or you need to have money. But if I could land this job, if it's not totally a scam, I could dust my hands off and leave these last few weeks behind. Space can't be any worse than my current life.

I slip out when the bell chimes for my lunch break. Space Rodeo Avenue is only minutes away.

Chapter Two

ASHER

"Why in the world did you put 'princess' wanted in the ad?" I look over at Helena, the stately secretary for our cowboy league.

She wiggles her brows and flips her long hair off one shoulder. "Royalty is very popular on Earth. Just take a look at the news down there. They're always talking about princess this and prince that and kings and queens. It's a big deal. And..." Pausing, she lifted both of her hands in the air, letting them fall in exasperation. "You need a princess."

I've visited Earth many times. Maybe royalty *is* in the news there, but the only royalty they have left there is in name only. No matter, Helena is right. I need a princess. "Fair enough. When does my ship leave?"

She lifts a hand in the air, tapping at what appears to be an invisible spot in front of her. It instantly reveals the scheduling screen. Our planet, Aphroditea, is a hub for intergalactic transport. Spaceships zip through here on the regular, arraying out through the galaxy. It makes for convenient travel. We are one of the first stops to and from Earth. Although Earth is struggling as a planet, it's still a popular place for travel. Many travelers are curious to see the planet trying to rebound from being almost destroyed by its own people.

"You can leave in an hour," Helena says with a satisfied smile. She clasps her hands together in front of her chest. "You are going to fall in love, Asher. I just know it."

"Here's to hoping," I reply with a light shrug.

I'm trying not to let the pressure get to me, but I kind of need to get married. Our people believe in this thing called infinity pulse. In short, true love with an intense physical connection.

Beyond my own need to find a mate, our planet *needs* women. It all started two years ago. We revere women on our planet so much that we hold an annual festival to honor them. Two years ago, a massive space storm blew through the area during the festival, and many women perished. Our kind has cross-mated with humans for centuries.

We've hatched a plan and put out a call on Earth. I'm technically a prince, for reals. If I do find a princess to mate with, part of the plan is that she will help find more women to mate with others on my planet. No pressure. At all.

We hope it will strengthen our numbers. Rumor has it, life on Earth isn't too great for women. Unlike our planet, where we revere women, they are frequently abused on Earth. During the decline in Earth's climate, women lost many rights, which set off a chain of events, thrusting women back to being treated like shadows. On Aphroditea, we put them on pedestals. For example, even though I'm a prince, I can't even call upon all my powers until I have a princess to share them with.

That's what makes this plan so critical for our people.

Chapter Three

JANE

I adjust my skirt, looking down at my feet in the elevator. I think I'm dressed professionally but attractively. That's a seriously fine line to walk. I'm wearing a powderpuff pink skirt that falls to my knees and flares slightly. Atop that is a cotton blouse with nice lines that smooths over my hips. I only hope I don't sweat too much by the time I get into this interview.

For over a century, humans have traveled to space. Yet it's mostly limited to those with the money to pay for the travel. The opportunity for a job off of Earth is unusual. Things aren't exactly great around here. Of course, there's my own life, which sucks, plus the baking-hot earth and being a woman. Plenty of men on earth hate women. They openly grouse about how awful we all are even though they hate us, so why should they care?

They still can't quite figure out why anyone would want to be with them. That's not even a rhetorical question.

I'd thought myself lucky to find Kyle. But now I'd lost him and my not-friend in one swoop.

The elevator chimes when it reaches the right floor. The musical chime sets my pulse to racing. I smooth my hands over my skirt, once again adjusting my purse over my shoulder as I step out and stride briskly down the hallway. I tend to walk fast when I'm nervous. Suite 7 on floor seven. I'm taking the repetition of numbers as a lucky sign.

I step into the quiet lobby to find a woman seated at the desk. She appears mostly human. I can't help but wonder, though. Rumor has it humans have cross-bred with aliens on other planets for centuries.

She smiles at me. "Can I help you?" Her voice is melodic and low.

Her hair is pulled back tightly and twisted into a braid spun into a tidy bun high on her head.

"I'm here for an interview," I say as I stop in front of the desk.

"Oh yes!" Her eyes brighten, and her smile widens. "You must be Jane." At my nod, she straightens her shoulders. "Excellent. I'm Helena. Have a seat. I will let him know you're here."

"Him?" I think to myself as I sit down in the only chair available.

I still wonder if this was really a joke. It was listed as an interview for a princess. It also said they were looking for someone skilled with matching people. Except for myself, I'm great at matchmaking. Even my ex-bestie ended up with my ex. I could even say I brought them together. We used to joke that they matched. Ha!

I'd also found halfway decent guys for some friends at work. I'm hoping my matchmaking skills will be my ticket. Because the princess part has to be a joke.

I'm getting all tangled up in my thoughts and nervous as hell. I pull out my phone and reread the ad.

I'd even saved my application, where I had, in my tipsy state, said, "I've always wanted to be a princess. I think I'm uniquely qualified. For starters, I love pink."

O.M.F.G.

"Jane?" the woman calls.

I look up. "Yes?" I stand quickly and slip my phone into my purse.

"Come on back." She rounds her desk, which is really just one of those folding plastic tables. It's a little old and battered, to be honest, but there are tons of them around. Since Earth started baking like a furnace, we've stopped producing many materials and now recycle many things. Those folding plastic desks are indestructible.

Helena leads me through a doorway and down a short hallway. I can't help but notice that we pass three offices, and all of them are empty. I have no idea what to think of that. I'm starting to wonder if my tipsy job application is some kind of scam.

Who would be hiring a princess anyway?

Seconds later, she stops by a doorway and opens it. "Here we are."

I step into the office to discover an imposing man there. Helena glances from me to him. "This is Asher. He'll be conducting your interview."

In a blink, she disappears, closing the door with a decisive click behind her.

Asher stands from where he's seated at a table. Two chairs are positioned on either side of a small round table with a pitcher of water and two glasses.

When I finally take a good look at him, my lungs seize, and I can barely breathe. He's *really* tall. I'm decidedly medium height, maybe five feet six inches if I stretch to my tallest.

This Asher guy has to be at least a foot and a half

taller than me. My eyes wander. His features are... well, the only word that comes to mind is fierce, which feels ridiculous, but it's accurate. His eyes are a bright starlight blue. His deeply bronzed skin almost shimmers under the dull glow of the fluorescent lights. As I study him, I conclude he isn't fully human. I wouldn't say he has scales, but he sort of does.

His eyes roam boldly over me, and I can practically feel the heat of his gaze like licks of fire on my skin.

"Jane," he finally says with a dip of his chin. His cheekbones are angled sharply down to a firm and well-defined mouth. He takes a step, turning to gesture toward a chair. It's only then I realize he has something like a tail.

When I step closer, my body feels electric, the sensation running like a current through me. This man arouses me intensely. I can feel the moisture between my thighs.

Whoa.

He holds his hand out when I step closer, and I reach to shake his hand. His touch is warm and dry and sends heat radiating up my arm. My body feels as if flames flicker through me like little bonfires lighting across the surface of my skin.

I swallow as I look up at him. His shoulders are broad, and he's wearing some sort of leather. I'm not really sure. He gives off the vibe of a cowboy. Except maybe I'm thinking that because the ad said it was looking for a "princess for a space cowboy."

"Are you a space cowboy?" I blurt out.

Those piercing blue eyes hold mine, and he lifts one shoulder in an insouciant shrug. "That's the best way to describe me, probably." His lips quirk, one side kicking up higher than the other.

My belly does a little flip, and a gush of moisture floods my panties.

"Would you like to sit down?" he prompts.

I try to stay focused, but what I really want to do is kiss him. I thought this whole thing was a joke. It has to be. My intense response must be because I got dumped by my fiancé and lost my best friend all in one swoop.

I decide to approach this directly. What do I have to lose, after all?

"Is this a joke? Do you really need a princess? And what planet are you from?" I ask, my questions tumbling out in a rush.

I literally can't look away from him. My belly fills with butterflies as my pulse gallops at a breakneck pace.

"It's definitely not a joke." His voice is all rumbly. I like it.

"You actually need a princess?" I prompt. "And who is the prince?"

"Me."

Chapter Four

ASHER

Jane's stunning green eyes widen as she stares up at me. I've met plenty of human women before. They've been traveling to our planet for centuries.

But I've never met any woman who I want the way I want Jane. Arousal chases through my system so fast my entire body feels like a live wire. Because my people are descended from humans, we've always been able to mate with them. We evolved and mated with those on our planet when we were first brought there two centuries ago.

I have never mated with a human. But I've also never been pledged to any woman. I've only had passing encounters. I tell myself that is why I want Jane so badly.

I take in her tousled brown curls and plump cheeks with freckles. Her mouth parts slightly, and her pink tongue darts out to slide across her bottom lip. I need to kiss her. I need more than that. The need is like static in my brain, drowning out other thoughts.

"*You* are the prince?" Her voice is raspy and throaty.

I could listen to her all day. I want to hear her call my name when I make her body sing for me, just me.

"Yes," I say as I step closer, forgetting that we're supposed to do some kind of interview here.

This *is* a job, after all. I need her to be my princess so we can ascend to the throne of king and queen when needed.

She takes a step closer as I move toward her. We're standing immediately in front of each other. It's as if a force field surrounds us, humming with the electricity of our connection. This is how it's supposed to happen.

For my people, when you find your mate, *your fated*, you can experience the elusive infinity pulse. I've been told it's like a song where you can feel the vibration between you. One body calls to the other. Though my parents have it, I've always been skeptical because not everyone finds it.

I reach for Jane, sliding my arm around her waist, thinking she may resist. But she doesn't. She steps closer, and a little growl escapes from my throat when I feel her soft, plush curves barely pressing against my body. My fingers splay just at that sweet dip of her waist, and I can feel the curve of her bottom.

"Do you know what this is?" I rasp.

Her cheeks are flushed pink, her eyes dark with desire. "I'm not sure. I know I want you," she says with a lift of her chin.

I answer with a dip of my head as I lean down and breathe in her scent. She smells sweet, a little sugary. I want to taste her, all of her. My mouth waters. "Can I kiss you?" I nearly growl.

My cock aches for her, and I want to mate her now, to fill her with my seed and make her plump with our baby.

But I can't go that far, not even close. That has to wait until we're on my planet.

"Please," she whispers.

I take another breath before I press my lips to the side of her neck in a hot, open-mouthed kiss. I love the way she trembles and arches against me. I can feel the hard points of her nipples against my chest. She's all softness against the hard planes of my body.

I lift my head to find her staring up at me, her lips parted and pink. I can feel her racing pulse where my thumb has come to rest at the base of her throat.

Her tongue swipes across her bottom lip again, and she says, "Kiss me."

"As you wish," I say just before I bring my lips to hers.

It's a brushing tease, and then her tongue darts out. I can't help myself anymore, and I fit my mouth over hers, sliding my hand over the soft, sweet curve of her bottom. I pull her against me, feeling a surge of gratification at the way she gasps into our kiss. I know she can feel my arousal pressing against her low belly. Our tongues twine, and our kiss goes on and on and on.

I'm teetering on the edge of my control when I force myself to break away. We stare at each other. My breath is coming in deep heaves.

"I need to say something," I bite out.

"Anything," she says.

I nudge her backward and lift her onto the desk. Her skirt rides up around her hips. I push her thighs apart, my eyes on her the entire time. Her legs are bare, her skin pink and flushed all over.

"Asher..."

I lift my gaze to hers. "Yes?"

"What's happening?"

"You are mine, and I am yours. Don't worry. We won't go too far today. I just have to see something."

I push her knees a little farther apart, my eyes flicking down to see her panties drenched with her desire. She's so wet that her arousal coats the insides of her thighs.

My cock throbs, and I can feel my seed leaking out the tip. I cup my palm over her mound, pressing into the fabric. She whimpers as her hips rock into my touch.

"I cannot fill you until we're on my planet," I say, nearly groaning with need. "But I want you to come for me."

Jane takes a shaky breath and nods. I drag her panties down her legs to see her pretty, glistening pink pussy. I tease my fingers in it, sliding them inside to fill her.

Her eyes are on mine as she says, "I need to see you too. It's only fair." I love how she's sassy and bold.

She reaches for the ties on my breeches, giving a little yank as they unravel. My cock, swollen with need for her, *only her*, springs free. I feel cum roll out the tip down to the base.

It doesn't matter, not completely, but I have one question for her. "Have you ever mated with a man before?"

Pain and bitterness flash in her eyes. I don't even know who hurt her, but I'm angry on her behalf.

"I was saving myself, but he betrayed me."

"Oh, sweetheart, I love knowing that," I rasp. More cum rolls out of the tip of my cock.

It's going to take all of my restraint not to fill her. "You're going to be my princess, so I can't take that from you, not yet. Not until we're on my planet, not until we are mated and married. Have you ever come?"

"Not with anyone else," she says.

Our people worship women, deeply and completely.

I've heard that men on Earth are selfish and don't always make sure women are taken care of. I'll find out more about who betrayed her. But for now, I'll make her come, and my seed will drip all over her pussy.

"You will now," I say.

I tease my fingers through her folds and pump them into her as her hips rock toward me. She looks down at my cock where my seed drips out.

"Someday, I will fill you with that," I say, as I wrap my other hand around it, sliding it up and down.

Her chest heaves as she stares at me, her eyes flicking down to my cock. I feel a surge of arousal inside her pussy.

"Please," she whispers.

Here is this woman, all woman, deeply aroused as her pussy throbs around my fingers.

All I want is to be inside her, but that will have to wait. For now, I tug her hips close to the edge of the desk, watching as I bring the tip of my thick cock to nestle between her slick, swollen folds. We watch together as I slide up and down, her arousal mingling with mine. Her plump little clit presses out against my shaft.

She's whimpering and panting. "Oh, Asher," she moans. "Please."

I continue rocking my hips, angling just enough to create friction over that sweet spot. Her hands clasp the edge of the desk as she arches back, her entire body trembling until I feel her pussy clenching.

It's all I can do not to fill her, but I cling to my control. "Look at me," I say.

Her eyes lift to mine, and that pulse shimmers between us.

Chapter Five

JANE

I feel filthy and aroused beyond measure as my orgasm slams through my body with wave after wave of sharp, intense pleasure. I feel him watching me as the tip of his cock teases over my slippery folds. For a head-spinning moment, I think he's going to fill me, but he doesn't. Even though that's what I want more than anything.

Asher holds me close. All the while, my heartbeat rampages in my chest, and I try to scramble for some sense of control. His touch is soothing and protective at once. I want to stay there forever, warm in his arms. I have no idea how much time has passed when there's a sharp knock on the door.

"Your Highness?" a voice called.

I leaned back, the knock and the strange way he was addressed puncturing the haze in my brain.

"Your Highness?" I stared up at him.

Chapter Six

ASHER

Jane has this cute little wrinkle between her brows. She blinks up at me as she slides her hips off the desk. I'm disappointed when her skirt falls to cover her thighs. I have to drag my brain back into gear. I shrug as I step back from her.

"I'll explain. Just a moment," I say.

I cross the room and peer around the edge of the door. "Still interviewing."

Helena smiles up at me. "I like her. How's it going?" Her whisper is close to a shout.

I bite back a laugh. "Well. I'll be out soon."

After closing the door again, I turn and look over at Jane. She's still standing by the table and looks delectably flustered. Her cheeks are pink, and her lips swollen from our kiss.

I have a whole line of interviews set up today, but I know that I'm going to cancel all of them. Jane will be my princess. I just have to explain it to her now. Well, that and the matchmaking job.

As I approach her again, she puts her hands on her hips, lifting her chin a little and narrowing her eyes.

"Do you normally kiss people at interviews? It's highly unprofessional, you know." Her tone is a little prim.

I stop in front of her, my hands literally itching to touch her again with need's claws sharpening.

My lips tug into a smile as I study her. "I don't usually kiss people at interviews. It's just—" I stop abruptly, taking a moment to collect myself. "I know you feel it too," I finally say.

"The ad is for a matchmaker," she points out.

I'm relieved she gives me the opening I need to get this interview back on track. I gesture to one of the chairs. "Have a seat. I'll explain everything."

Jane sits, smoothing her hands over her skirt. *All I want is to see her with her knees spread open for me. Again.*

Shackling my rampaging arousal, I sit down in the other chair, facing her at an angle. "The ad *is* for a matchmaker, and I also need a princess."

"I wondered if that part was some kind of joke? I'll be perfectly honest now that we've kissed. I had several glasses of wine before I saw the ad. If I'd been sober, I probably wouldn't have applied. Are you really from another planet? And why do you need a princess? Royalty is just fluff on Earth."

I nod. "I am from another planet. While I look mostly human, I'm not entirely. Our people have mated with humans from Earth for centuries. We are aware that life on Earth isn't great these days, especially for women. I understand things have only gotten worse. It's very dry and inhospitable. Are the rumors accurate about the way women are treated here?"

Jane purses her lips. She nods, and something flashes in her eyes. Pain, I think. I want to slay all of her dragons, including whoever hurt her.

"We lost many rights. With the climate changing,

things got even worse because many women died. Is it just as bad on your planet?"

"Women are revered on our planet. When you look at history everywhere, not just on Earth, there are differing reactions when change happens. Taking rights away when things become scarce, or protecting rights when things become scarce. Our people protect and revere women because we need them. A bad storm two years ago caused many women to die. We need women, and we can mate with humans. It strengthens us." I take a quick breath. "As for the princess part. Some of our people think royalty is revered here because of what's in your news. But I'm not so sure that's accurate."

Jane's eyes widen. "I guess it depends on how you look at it." Her lips twist with a smile. "Royalty is honored on Earth, but they don't have real power. So if you're a prince, why is there no princess?"

When I shake my head, she circles her hand in the air. "Why not?"

"There will be. I need a princess so I can ascend to the throne as king when my father is ready to step down. I must find my princess, and I need a match-maker. We want to set up a service where we match women with the men who need them. We know there are plenty of women here. With Earth being so unfriendly, we thought it might be appealing to move to our planet. It would be—"

"A match made in space," Jane quips with a grin.

"Exactly. Maybe that's what we should call it," I tease.

"Yes!" She claps her hands before giving her head a little shake and lowering them. "How many interviews do you have? And are you going to kiss everyone?"

"If you want the job, it's yours," I say firmly. "I need to clarify one thing."

"What?" She leans forward, clasping her hands on her knees as she looks at me.

"We need to marry once we land on my planet, and then we must consummate the marriage quickly. Normally, I wouldn't rush, but we have to. Things are in flux, and if I don't take a princess soon, someone else may become the prince."

"When do we need to leave?"

"Tomorrow."

Chapter Seven

JANE

I blink at Asher. I don't realize my mouth has dropped open until he reaches across and nudges my chin upward with his knuckles. That little brushing touch is like fire on my skin. It's electric. I don't even know what to think of my reaction to him. It's so intense, I'd say it's out of this world, but that feels ridiculous, given the circumstances.

"Tomorrow?" I squeak.

Asher's shoulders rise as he takes a breath and nods. "Today."

"Are you sure?"

"Absolutely," he says solemnly. "Have you ever traveled to space?"

I shake my head slowly as a mix of anticipation, anxiety, and fear rushes through me.

"Only the wealthy can do that. I'm definitely not that. Were you looking for someone with money?" My question is cynical, but that's life on Earth these days for women. Most men are looking for connections or money.

He waves a hand dismissively. "Money is irrelevant.

I didn't know how long it would take me to find the right woman. I'm just glad I found you."

"How do you know it's me?"

He reaches over, curling his big hand over both of mine where they're clasped on my knees. Energy races through me in a loop, fiery and intense.

"Do you feel that?" he asks.

I can barely breathe as I nod with a sense of connection and intimacy surging through me, almost its own force. "What does that mean?" I whisper.

"That is what my people call infinity pulse. It only happens if we're meant to be mated, and not everyone finds their one true mate."

"It's not just lust?" I can't help but ask.

Asher's intense blue eyes hold mine as he shakes his head slowly. "This isn't just lust. Have you felt lust before?"

Fair question. I'd felt a dim shadow of what this was but nothing more.

"So we travel to your planet and marry. Then?" I prompt.

"I think that might be the easy part," he says. "Then you set up a matchmaking service. You will need to travel to and from Earth until you decide if you prefer to have someone else handle it here."

"How many men on your planet need brides?"

"Many," he says.

Chapter Eight

ASHER

Jane stares at me. "Well?" I prompt. I'm trying to wrestle my body's powerful response to her under control.

She takes a quick breath. "I'll do it."

Satisfaction surges inside me. I traveled here hoping to find my bride, but this with Jane is so much more than I expected. I was prepared to compromise. To simply find someone suitable. But for us to truly be linked? It was all I wanted. *She* is all I want.

"What do I need to do now?" she asks.

"We need Helena."

I stand quickly, and I'm about to walk to the door when I turn back. Jane stands and starts to follow me. I stop in front of her, reaching for both of her hands. "The next few days will feel rushed, but I promise you it will be okay."

She blinks at me. "Okay."

Chapter Nine

JANE

I stand in my apartment that evening, looking around at the tiny space. I'm about to leave not only this apartment but also this entire freaking planet.

O.M.G.

There's moving, and then there's what I'm about to do.

My cell phone vibrates on the table, jangling with a distinct harsh ring I've set for only one person. Part of me had wanted to block Kylie's number, but I'd opted against that. I need the reminder so my anger stays alive.

I cross the room to glance down at the screen. Kylie never has the nerve to leave a voicemail, but she always texts after she calls. I don't answer.

True to form, a text follows after the phone stops ringing. *You have to know how sorry I am. Please call me. He's cheating on me.*

I snort.

In a welcome change, the anger burning like a hot coal inside me over her betrayal barely registers. It's still there, tangled with bitterness. I don't know if trust will ever come easily for me again. Yet those moments with Asher have shifted something inside me.

I'm still not sure if the job isn't a massive joke on me, but I don't think it is.

I let my gaze arc around my little apartment once more. In the months following the blowup of my engagement, I'd hated this apartment. I had hopes and dreams. Kyle and I were going to try to buy a house together. Maybe it wouldn't have been amazing, because life on Earth wasn't all that amazing these days. But we had been vying to get into the green belt area where things were a little better than the desert conditions on most of Earth.

Instead, Kyle screwed my friend, and I'd felt trapped in my tiny apartment, knowing that my chances of finding something new and moving on were limited. And now, all because I had a few too many glasses of wine and recklessly applied for a job, I just might be moving on. In a major way.

I ignore the text from Kylie. She's made her own bed, and she can lie in it alone, just like I've been doing for months.

I swipe past her text and pull up the information Helena sent me. My thoughts spin back to the meeting with her after that crazy-wild kiss with Asher. Helena gave me the job details and sent over more information about their planet.

I'm meeting with her tomorrow morning to confirm the travel details. I can't wait.

———

Helena smiles at me from across the table. It was only

after I'd looked through all the information she'd sent me that I realized she wasn't fully human.

She's tall and pretty and intimidating with sharp features and a slender tail. "Jane?" she prompts.

"Oh, yes?" My wandering thoughts aren't helping move the conversation along.

"What did you think?"

"The planet looks beautiful," I say.

"It *is* beautiful," Helena says, her tail snapping like a tiny whip. "It is similar to how Earth used to be. With some differences, of course."

Before we destroyed the environment, many areas on Earth were green and lush. Now, Earth is like a giant desert with a few tiny pockets of fresh water and plants.

"Where will I be living?" I ask.

I'm honestly game for anything. I feel so free. I have nothing to keep me here.

"You will live in Lapis Loch, the capital of our planet. There are mountains and a lake nearby. I'm confident you will love it." Her gaze shifts to look out the grimy window. The wind blows sand through the air, and no speck of green is visible. "I do believe you will find our environment more welcoming than here," Helena says.

These days, life on Earth was rather grim, just one endless hot day.

"We have seasons as well, including snow in the winter," she adds.

Excitement bubbles in my chest, and I clasp my hands together. "So, um, Asher said you would explain the matchmaking job?"

"Yes. Two years ago, we had a massive storm. Our people revere women, and we hold an annual festival to celebrate them. Lots of women were at the festival, which was hit hard by the storm. As a result, many women perished." Helena lifts her chin, deep sadness flickering in her gaze. "We need more women for mates. Our people have mated with humans for centuries. We intend to set up a matchmaking service here on Earth." She pauses, a glint of humor entering her gaze. "I understand from Asher that perhaps the bit about royalty might've been a little much in the ad?" Her eyes twinkle.

Laughter bubbles in my throat, but I try to hold it back until she adds, "Go ahead and laugh."

I laugh softly. "It's not that royalty isn't a thing here. It is, but it's mostly in the tabloids, which are sort of junky news. Royalty hasn't been anything real for a long time, even before Earth became what it is now. I always wanted to be a princess when I was a little girl." I shrug sheepishly. "But it wasn't anything I could ever plan on." I feel my old childish excitement rise inside. "Is royalty not a joke on your planet?"

Helena studies me before nodding, her expression shifting to solemn. "Absolutely. Asher's parents are the current king and queen of our planet. Asher must find a princess, or his rightful role as the heir to the throne can be challenged. This may seem like a lot, but you must marry and consummate the marriage on the same day you arrive on our planet. Are you ready for that?"

I stare at her with my heart about to beat its way out of my chest. So many questions bounce around in my thoughts, and I don't even know where to begin. I think briefly about my life here. I have no one here. The idea of being somewhere new is wildly appealing, even if I'm afraid.

"I realize there's no way to get all my questions answered," I finally say. Just as I begin, there's a sharp knock on the door. I don't know how a single knock can be commanding, but it is.

Helena stands immediately as Asher steps into the room. I know it's him without even looking because I can *feel* the voltage of his presence. It's like an electric charge vibrating in the air between us as I turn to glance over my shoulder.

That intense attraction, twined within an unfamiliar emotion, shimmies to life between us. Our eyes meet. While I still have a gazillion questions, my doubts burn in the ashes of the heat of our connection.

Okay, maybe that sounds corny, but it's true.

I take a quick breath, glancing back at Helena. "I'm ready," I say with more confidence than I feel. About the only thing I feel confident in is Asher. Maybe I shouldn't place my trust and faith in an alien space cowboy, but I do.

Chapter Ten

ASHER

A mere day later, Jane stands beside me, nervously clutching a small bag. My eyes coast over her. Her hair is pulled up in some kind of twist with a few wayward brown curls dangling around her cheeks. Her skin is flushed, and her tongue darts out nervously to slide across her bottom lip. Lust sizzles inside, cracking through my system like a whip through the air.

"Um, how does this work?" she asks, puncturing my thoughts.

I don't want to talk at the moment. What I want to do is carry her away and keep her all to myself until I get enough of her to slake the need rampaging through me. However, what I *must* do is get her on our transport and back to Aphroditea as swiftly as possible.

The deadline for me to find a princess has created some scuffles on our planet. An uprising in a smaller town has been vying to intercede in the order of succession.

I don't care about power for the sake of power, but I do care about the fate of my family and our people.

We must keep our tribes and people strong. Ever since humans came to our planet centuries prior, some saw it as weakening our people. A small and noisy faction in another town has been trying to strike out and take over. They call themselves purists, yet they are dying as a result.

My family has led our planet for centuries. We claim the throne, and we have presided over the safety and protection of our planet without fail. I must return quickly and marry within hours of landing.

"Asher?" Jane's voice interjects.

I bring my focus to her. I step closer and reach for her hand, curling mine around it. I can't help myself. I need to touch her. Lifting her hand, I turn it over, dropping a kiss in the center of her palm and nuzzling that sweet, soft skin inside her wrist. Goose bumps rise on her skin, and I can feel her shiver. I bring my eyes to hers as I lift my head.

"We take the fastest transport to Aphroditea. Normally, we coordinate with the collective transport among the planets because it's more convenient, but we need to move quickly, so we're taking one for leaders only. We will arrive on my planet in a few hours."

Jane blinks up at me. "Okay," she says, her voice a little breathless.

A single word in her voice quickens the drumbeat of need inside. I can't wait for so many things with her.

The next hour is a rush to get situated with transport. Once we are traveling, Jane and I are in a private suite. Questions spill out of her. She wants to know about the food, the weather, so many things. She's also worried about learning a new language. I quickly explain that our people speak English. "There are other languages," I add, "but on our planet, we speak primarily English and French."

"French?" she prompts, her brows rising.

I nod. "Yes. When the cowboys from the United States were recruited there to mate and strengthen the health of our ancestors, there were also French cowboys from the same era, known as gardians. Our people's original language is spoken by some. I suppose you could think of it like the old tribal languages in so many areas centuries ago."

"Oh, this is so interesting. Obviously, we learned about our own history and traveling to other planets, but I didn't know this. Why were cowboys recruited to your planet?"

"You'll find many aliens travel among planets and mate. Cowboys have always been nomadic. At the time, people from Earth were looking for safe havens; many came, and some of the languages became primary."

Jane nods slowly. "Do you speak French?"

"Oui," I reply.

Her cheeks flush. "I know a little bit of French. That was the language I took in high school, but I haven't had much chance to use it since then."

I can't help myself. I lean over to brush my lips over hers. I've been keeping my need for her on a tight leash. We have to wait to consummate until after our marriage ceremony.

When her sweet tongue glides against mine and I hear the little whimper in the back of her throat, I have to lift my head. "Soon," I promise.

———

We arrive on my planet, and Jane stands from her seat as soon as I do. She looks around for her bag. "Should I —"

"Your belongings will be taken to our home."

Her eyes are wide as we step off the transport. It's a beautiful day on our planet. She looks around, her eyes alight with wonder. I follow her gaze, absorbing what, for her, is entirely new.

Our planet's capital, Misti, is lush and green. There are mountains to the side with a blue mist shimmering over them. Green trees with silver moss surround a nearby lake, which is deep blue and glimmers under our sun. Our planet's sun isn't as hot or bright as Earth's sun.

A large bird calls, and Jane's eyes seek it out. "That is called a green heron," I offer. "It's related to the herons that used to be on Earth. Our environment is very similar. Like humans, wildlife also travels. There are some differences, though."

At that moment, there is a flash of brown to the side. "What's that?"

I glance over. "That's a wild hare. They're every-where here and similar to hares and rabbits from Earth, but much larger."

Before we can talk further, we are surrounded by a bustle of activity. Someone is getting Jane's bag and directing us away. We are swept up into the official events, already organized before our arrival. Helena had sent notice back that I'd found my princess. My parents arrive, and I gesture toward Jane.

"This is Jane," I say to my mother.

My mother, Alisha, dips her head as she stops in front of Jane.

Jane has already asked if she needs to curtsy, and I explained that she does not. Although our family is royal, we don't stand on ceremony. Our power is derived from caring for our people and our planet.

My mother holds out her hand as the customary greeting on Earth. After she shakes Jane's hand, my mother steps back, studying her for a few beats. She looks over at me. "You chose well."

My father, Ash, confers with Helena, and he steps away, giving me a quick embrace before he turns to Jane. His keen gaze takes her in. I see his glint of acknowledgment and pride when he glances at me.

"Very nice to meet you, Jane," he says, clasping her hand quickly.

Jane looks nervous. My father holds her hand for another moment, assuring her, "A lot is happening, and we understand it may feel overwhelming. It will all be well. Once the ceremony is over, you and Asher will be able to go to your home and have a week to yourselves."

Jane nods. There isn't time for a casual chat. We are swept away, with my mother quickly explaining the process to Jane. My mother had also come here from Earth, but that was some thirty-odd years ago now.

Unlike our situation, she had met my father when he was on Earth for a tour. He had fallen for her instantly.

Like Jane, she was wise and recognized the fate of women on Earth, where they were treated poorly and the environment was terrible for humans. It's a struggle unless you are wealthy there.

A short while later, we enter the royal emporium. It's something like a church for our people, but not quite.

My mother takes Jane aside to get her ready for the ceremony. I watch as they disappear, sensing Jane's anxiety. It seems the only time she is calm is when we're touching. Fortunately, there will be plenty of that soon.

As soon as Jane dresses in the wedding gown my mother has ready for her, my mother assured me we will have a few minutes alone in the vestibule before the ceremony. My heart is casting out impatient beats.

————

A short while later, Jane stares at me, her lips kiss swollen and her eyes wide. My fingers are buried inside her, and my cum drips down over her pussy. We've done everything except the final act. I look down to see my seed dripping down my shaft and over her pink core. I cannot wait to fill her later, to breed her.

She stares at me. She's still trembling. It takes everything in me to step back from her. I lift her silk panties off the floor. She shimmies her hips off the table. I slide her panties over her hips, satisfied to discover the silk is instantly wet from my seed. She lets out a little whimper when I cup my palm over her mound, and we stand there for a moment. "More later, I promise."

Chapter Eleven

JANE

I still can't believe I'm even here. Asher's eyes hold mine, and it's the only comfort I can find in the tumult of the last few days of my life.

He is saying his vows. I hear him promise to protect me, to care for me, and pledge his love to me. Moments later, I repeat back everything to him.

The words are a blur, and it's as if it's all a dream. At the same time, it feels more real than anything. I'm caught in the beam of Asher's intent gaze, and I don't want to look away.

My heart beats strong and true with every word. When the officiant pronounces us bound by our vows and officially married, I feel the hot shock of Asher's lips on mine. The reality becomes physical.

There's a little cheer in the room, the sound echoing around us. I almost forget where we are until Asher lifts his head, his eyes instantly holding mine again. "How are you?" he asks, his tone low.

Heat rolls through me in waves, and my pulse races. It feels like hooves pounding through me.

"Good," I answer. Because it's true, and I don't

know what other word to use to describe the enormity of what I'm feeling.

I'm literally on another planet, now officially married to the prince of this world.

"Princess Jane," Asher's mother says as she approaches.

She's dressed officially, crown and all. I'm startled to discover she's setting a tiara on my head. "What?" I sputter.

"You are now the princess of our people," she says calmly.

Okay, wow. I take a shaky breath, and Asher's hand slides down my arm, his strong touch easing the emotions storming through me.

He lifts my hand, dropping a kiss in the center of my palm as I take another unsteady breath. His mother had told me just before the ceremony that many events would happen in quick succession after the official marriage.

She leads the way as we begin to walk. I glance around at the crowd. Some look entirely human, and others are more like Asher, taller with tails of varying lengths and skin almost like shimmery gold. Guards flank us as we walk in an orderly procession out of this place that seems like a church.

The air is warm and soft outside, and the sun is bright. Asher holds my hand, bending low to say in my ear, "We will be able to go to our home soon."

"Okay." I promised myself this morning I would just go with the flow since this is all so new to me.

We walk through an archway of beautiful flowers. I marvel at seeing actual flowers for the first time in my entire life. We walk alongside a river where birds are chirping nearby until we reach a gated area we're ushered through.

Asher bends low to tell me, "This is my family's area. Our home is over there." He gestures toward a winding path that rises over a hill. "We can't see the house from here. You'll see it this afternoon. I hope you love it."

Whenever I look into Asher's eyes, my feelings are pure, raw emotion. I think it's love, but I don't really know. It's so different from how I felt about my ex.

Through the gate is a beautiful garden area with walls surrounded by tall trees that appear to serve as a natural protection. Long tables contain food, and people and aliens are everywhere.

I'm introduced to what seems like hundreds of others. Asher's parents, the king and queen, are seated at the head of a table, and Asher and I are seated at another table nearby. We are feted with toasts, and the food is delicious. I'm used to rations on Earth, which are simply enough but no more due to the constant supply issues.

It's strange to see and taste so many foods. "Everything is delicious," I say to Asher at one point. I'm too nervous to eat much, but I do enjoy trying new things.

He smiles down at me, leaning over to give me a lingering kiss. My heart beats faster, my pulse wild and uncontrolled. I wonder how long it will take me to get used to him, to get used to feeling like this. I wonder if the intensity will start to fade.

I also wonder if I'll ever get used to this life. I glance around, my eyes landing on Helena. She's deep in conversation with an older man at a table nearby. She catches my eye and smiles encouragingly.

A sense of festiveness permeates the area until a group of men enters. One of them casts a glowering look over the crowd. I watch as they walk in what appears to be a formation with two men leading and four flanking them at an angle behind them. They stop in front of our table.

Asher glances up, his eyes narrowing. "Yes?"

A frisson of fear races down my spine. I don't know why, but I sense a threat from these men. Asher reaches for my hand under the table, lacing his fingers through mine with his thumb moving in a soothing pass along the edge of my wrist.

The man in the front studies me before his eye shifts to Asher. "Felicitations on your marriage," he says slowly.

Asher holds his gaze, lifting his chin slightly. "Thank you. This is Princess Jane." He releases my hand, sliding his arm around my shoulder before gesturing toward the man. "This is Honnell. He is from Silver, a town on the other side of the planet."

Honnell looks back at me. "Greetings, Jane."

Although I kind of think it's silly that everyone is calling me "princess" today, I mentally clock that he doesn't.

I sense tension begin to emanate from Asher. "She is *our* princess."

"Oh, come on," Honnell says. "Princess Jane."

It feels as if an entire conversation happens in front of me without many words. All kinds of undercurrents zip through the air. The men leave, and Asher seems to relax again. I'm beginning to get tired. Between the excitement and utter insanity of being on a new planet and getting married to a sexy alien space cowboy, it's a lot for me to absorb.

The party gradually breaks up, and Asher's parents come over. Even though I can't believe I'm technically a princess, I have to resist the urge to call her queen.

We stand off to the side of the tables near the arched entrance into this lovely garden. Asher's father levels his gaze with Asher's. "Do not worry about Honnell. He's been stirring up trouble for months. Now that you're married, it doesn't matter anymore."

"I know," Asher says simply.

Something passes between Asher and his father, and I have no idea how to interpret it. I don't think about it for long because he takes my hand and leads me away. Only moments later, he walks us along a pathway. I'm coming to realize that a security detail slips back as we walk through another archway into another walled area where a door closes behind us.

Asher glances down at me, stopping on the stone pathway lined with beautiful flowers.

"Inside these walls, it's just us unless we choose to bring someone in."

He gestures to the walls, and I realize they tower high into the sky. He points farther up. "There's a shield above us. Any break in it, and we'll be alerted instantly along with the security team."

I study him. "I think you and Helena and your mother tried to prepare me, but I didn't realize how much security there would be for us."

He shrugs lightly, adding, "It's just part of my life, and it's not all the time. It's only been recently because I hadn't married yet, and there was a threat to the order of succession. We keep some things in place no matter what, but it won't be so stressful in a few months when everyone has accepted our marriage. Come with me."

He reaches for my hand again, and we walk together off the pathway through a doorway. Despite all the pomp and circumstance around our marriage, the house is simple and not too ostentatious. It blends into the beautiful landscape. It is a single-story dwelling built into the edge of a hillside. When we enter, Asher takes me on a quick tour. Four sections create a square with a courtyard in the center.

He explains how the electricity for their entire planet comes from solar power from their sun. The stunning courtyard has a small pond filled with fish and is surrounded by lush green trees. A sweet scent drifts through the air.

"What is that smell?" I ask.

He gestures to a cluster of large pink flowers. "These are similar to peonies from Earth."

I lean close and inhale the heady, sweet fragrance. "Beautiful. I saw some flowers in our history books, but I've never seen any on Earth." When I meet his gaze again, I blurt out my anxious question, "Who are those men?"

"The men who want to challenge the throne. I'm married now, so it's okay. Only two more things have to happen."

"Consummation?" I prompted.

His lips kick up at the corners as he dips his head, and heat flares in his gaze. My belly shimmies.

"That and you must get pregnant."

My breath is shallow, and my pussy clenches. "How soon?" My voice comes out breathy and raspy. I never knew until Asher that I would desperately want to get pregnant.

"We must have an heir within eleven months."

"Oh."

"I think we can do that," he murmurs.

He steps closer and slides his palm around my waist. Seconds later, my body is flush with his. I can feel the hard, swollen length of him pressing against my lower belly.

"How much do you want me?" he asks, rocking his hips slightly.

I remember the feel of his fingers buried inside me and his cum damp on my panties before the wedding.

"So much," I whisper.

"Mmm." He nuzzles my neck, and his lips tease along the sensitive skin.

I feel as if I'm melting, tumbling into need and fire. His eyes hold mine, and I try to catch my breath.

Chapter Twelve

ASHER

Jane's eyes are dark, her cheeks are flushed pink, and I can feel the tight peaks of her nipples pressing through the silk of her dress. In all this time that I've looked for the woman who is to be mine, I'd begun to despair that I might ever feel what I believed could be possible. I'd begun to get practical, thinking I would settle for much less.

But now, I stare down at Jane, and I know she's dripping wet for me. I can't wait to bury myself in her tight pink pussy and fill her.

I can't wait for her to be carrying our child. I can't wait until her breasts are heavy with milk.

"Please," she whispers.

I finally kiss her, remembering how desperate I was for her right before the wedding and how wet she had been for me. I can feel the cum leaking out of the tip of my shaft. I made myself many promises earlier—about taking our time, going slow, not rushing, and so on. I don't want to keep any of them. I need to be inside her.

I lift my head, sucking in deep gulps of air. I tell her, "I need you. I want to go slow, but—"

My sassy wife says, "Don't you dare. Hurry, please."

She reaches between us and drags her palm over my thick length. Seconds later, we're tearing at each other's clothes, and I let out a little growl when she's finally naked. She's beyond beautiful. Her breasts are perky, her nipples a deep pink. I lean down to cup a breast, plumping it up and sucking her nipple into my mouth, savoring her sharp cry.

I lift my head and smooth my hand over the soft curve of her belly, delving between her thighs to find her hot and slick. I sink my fingers into her again. When I draw them out this time, I taste her, savoring the sweet tang of her arousal.

We haven't even gotten past the entryway to our home.

With every ounce of restraint I can find, I force myself to slow down. I have one arm banded around Jane's waist and the other sliding down over her shoulder. Her skin is silky and smooth, flushed pink with passion.

"Sweetheart," I rasp.

Jane's lashes lift, her eyes dark pools of desire. Her breath is coming in short, sharp little pants.

"What?" she asks in a ragged whisper.

"We should slow down," I say.

My cock disputes this point, pulsing where it presses against her belly. She blinks, and her tongue darts out to swipe across her bottom lip. She looks around where we are. The entry to our home is light and airy. Archways lead off to each side, one to the bedroom area and the other to the living room and kitchen.

I lift her in my arms, and she's a soft, naked bundle

of curves. I carry her into the living room, striding quickly over to a couch. I stretch her out on the couch, kneeling beside her. I take her in for a moment. She is *mine* now; we are bound.

Her curls are falling around her shoulders in a messy tumble. I let my eyes trail over her plump lips, down to take in her sweet breasts with her pink nipples ruched tightly. I slide my palm over the sweet curve of her belly, lingering for a moment over the curls nestled between her thighs before letting my hand trail down over the curve of her hip, along her leg, and slowly back up on the inside.

She shivers, and goose bumps rise on her skin. "Oh, sweetheart, it was worth the wait for this."

She lets out a breathy laugh. My eyes meet hers. "What's funny?"

"We only met two days ago," she points out.

"And I wanted all of you the moment I met you."

Her eyes get soft, and she bites her bottom lip. "I want all of you too," she whispers.

I gently press her knees apart. She's drenched with her arousal slick on the inside of her thighs. Her pussy is puffy, pink, and glistening. My cock throbs, and I cannot wait to fill her.

I tease my fingers into her soaking wet core, my eyes on her face as I sink two fingers inside her, knuckle deep.

"Have you been this wet since before the wedding?" I ask as I pump slowly in and out of her. She nods, a little whimper escaping from her throat. I can't wait any more and bring my mouth to her sex, tasting her as I fuck her with my fingers.

My restraint slips to the very end of its tether when I feel her trembling. I rise up. "I need to be inside you," I growl.

"Please, please... Asher, hurry," she begs.

I shift up onto the couch, stretching out over her and savoring the feel of her as I notch my thick crown at her entrance. "Jane," I say as her lashes begin to fall closed. Her eyes open. "You're my princess."

She blinks. "Ash—" she rasps, just as I bury myself inside her.

She's tight and clenching around me, and I'm already at the edge. I need to feel her find her pleasure first. I hold still, my voice on the edge of slurring as her legs curl around my hips and her hips rock toward mine.

Fused as closely as we can be, I feel like I've come home. I rise up on an elbow, brushing her tangled hair away from her face. I drop my forehead to hers and say, "Come for me, sweetheart."

She shudders underneath me, and I draw back to plunge in again, feeling the spurt of my seed filling her. She whimpers as I surge inside her, clinging to the thinnest thread of my control. I adjust the angle of my hips and reach between us to tease my fingers over her swollen clit.

She cries out, her entire body going taut and her pussy clamping around my length. I finally let go, my release coming in spurts as my mind nearly goes blank from the electricity sizzling through me.

Chapter Thirteen

JANE

I'm *made* of sensation. I feel Asher's release filling me as my own pleasure scatters like sparks through my entire body. All I know is an intense piercing pleasure so sharp it's on the edge of pain as my orgasm rocks me to my very core.

I savor his muscled weight above me, his thick length filling me and stretching me as he rocks back and sinks inside once more. I feel another burst of heat inside me.

He collapses over me and quickly shifts to roll us so that I'm splayed half over him. I'm utterly sated. His skin is warm. I let my fingertips trace over his chest, only now realizing that the surface is slightly scaled. It's just a shimmer, almost a trick of light.

I could stay here forever and don't ever want to leave. I rise up, wanting to look into his eyes. His gaze is heavy-lidded when his eyes meet mine. The blue is so deep that I almost feel it. I experience another shock, this one straight to my heart. I'm starting to understand what he meant when he said we were joined and what he meant about infinity pulse. Because this feeling is so intense, so powerful.

"I want to stay here forever," I say. I lift a hand to trace my fingertips along his collarbone.

"We could," he teases, his smile warm.

I feel his palm slide down my spine and over the curve of my bottom. He gives me a little squeeze. He's still inside me, and I feel him swell slightly.

"I'm sure we have things to do," I tease in return.

"We do." His fingertips move in a slow circle, tracing lazy paths on my bottom. "But we actually have a week to ourselves."

"Your mother mentioned that."

"We have one goal. I want you pregnant by the end of this week. That's why protocol dictates we stay here for the week. I understand on Earth your people once called it a honeymoon. We call it the week of pleasure. There is plenty of that, but there is an actual goal."

I feel heat rise into my cheeks. "Oh, well, I guess we'll be busy then. How will we get food and things?"

"The kitchen's already stocked for the week. Those serving us and guarding the home will continue with deliveries. No one will come inside the home. We won't need this much security long-term, but there's some concern until you're pregnant."

"What if I can't get pregnant?" I ask, a sense of worry sliding through me.

"The fertility for human women from Earth multiplies on our planet. You will get pregnant," he says as if stating a fact.

"You sound very confident," I say, a little surprised at this information.

"There has literally never been a human woman from Earth who didn't get pregnant within a month of arrival here after she's mated," Asher said, his tone calm.

He rocks his hips into mine, and I feel him swell inside me again. I'm a little startled to discover that I already feel arousal building within my body. My channel clenches around him, and his eyes hold mine as he rocks. He's fully aroused inside me now, his thickness stretching me.

"Oh!" A moan escapes.

His hands slide to grip my hips, and he rocks into me again. His cock is thick and long, and I love how he feels inside me. "Sit up and ride me," he tells me.

I can't believe the way I am with Asher. I feel no restraint. Our intimacy is pure. I don't hesitate. I straighten and straddle him.

His hands curve over my sides and grip my hips. "Watch," he says.

I look down, watching his thick length glistening from my arousal mingled with his cum. He fills me again and again as we watch together. It's filthy, and all I want is for him to fill me with his seed and make me plump with his baby.

My swollen clit pushes out. He adjusts his angle so that each time he sinks into me, there's a little friction right over my clit. I'm already chasing my release.

He says, "Come for me, sweetheart."

His thumbs press right where we're joined, and I cry out with my release, the sensation piercing and sharp. I feel him pumping into me slow and deep, his hot release filling me.

This time, I collapse on him. He holds me close, pressing tender kisses to my cheeks, his palm sliding down my back in a soothing caress.

When I finally manage to lift my head again, his

gaze is waiting for me. "Princess." His palm cups my cheek, and his thumb traces my bottom lip.

Chapter Fourteen

ASHER

The following morning, I wake up with Jane curled up lush and warm beside me. For a moment, I tell myself not to overdo it, not to constantly give in to the urges for her, which run as deep as a river.

But then, I remind myself we have a job this week. One that is nothing but pure pleasure for me. When I smooth my hand down over her side, I can't help but linger under the plump curve of her breast. She murmurs something sleepy, her eyes slowly opening as she rolls her head to the side.

"Do you call it morning here?" she asks, her voice soft, the edges crushed from sleep.

I feel my lips quirking up at the corners, savoring how her own smile curves against her cheek in return.

"Yes, we do." I dip my head and breathe in her scent.

I'm not sure how much later it is, but it's been a while. After I've teased her to climax, after we've lounged in bed, and after I took her again in the shower. She looks over at me while she's toweling off.

"It doesn't look like you have to worry about water supply here," she comments.

"Oh no. That's never an issue here. I haven't stayed long enough on Earth to worry, but I understand it's rationed there."

She nods. "It has been my whole life. From what I understand, it became dry in certain areas first. In the United States, it was out West. The rivers began to dry up, and the drought slowly spread east. East is where the green zone is now. I've never been there, though."

"Here, we have something sort of like a rainforest, but not quite as rainy. On the other side of the mountains, it's a little dryer., But even there, we never worry about water supply."

"Water can only run for three minutes or less on Earth," Jane says. "They put timers on all of the lines. They started doing that when people ignored the voluntary limits."

"I think you'll like it here. The environment is very similar to Earth before it got dry and fiery there."

"How often will I go back for the matchmaking?" she asks me.

"After this week, you will coordinate with our team that goes to Earth every other month. You will establish a plan. I presume every other month, but maybe not. Depends on how you set it up."

Jane's eyes twinkle as she tugs on some clothing. She has a swirly skirt and a tank top that stretches over her curves.

I don't even want to get dressed, but my body needs food, so I reluctantly pull on a shirt and breeches. Most of our clothing is similar to Earth but more practical. Although our environment here is better, and we have more luxuries, we've learned what not to do from other neighboring planets. We don't want to end up like them, with the environment nearly destroyed and manufacturing limited as a result.

"Come," I say after we're dressed, holding out a hand. "I'll give you a tour. This will be your home."

Her soft hand is warm in mine as I lead her out of her shower area. "Well, the bedroom and shower are lovely," she offers with a grin.

I pause and glance around the space. We have a large bedroom with a square bed with silky white fabric draped around the corners. The windows that face the inner courtyard are open, and a soft breeze gusts through. Brightly colored rugs decorate the floor on either side of the bed. The bathroom has the same glossy wooden flooring with a large open shower, a skylight above, and a soaking tub beside it. Many of our amenities are similar to Earth, primarily because we have intermingled with humans for centuries.

I lead her out of the bedroom along the hall that faces the inner courtyard. "This side is just our bedroom," I offer.

I turn to go around the back to one of the other sides of the square home, which houses our two offices. "Mine," I offer. "And yours."

"Oh!" she squeaks. "I have an office?"

"Oh yes. You'll be busy. While my family leads, we work very hard. You'll see."

We round the other corner, which is the main living space for us. The large sunken living room has a big couch and a small fireplace on the wall facing the home's outer area. The inside walls are lined with windows facing the inner courtyard. We turn into the last area, which is the kitchen.

"If you like to cook, we have a nice kitchen," I say as I swing my arm in an arc.

"Have you been living here all along?" she asks. She looks around, her eyes wide.

"No, the space has been waiting for me to be married. I can show you where I lived before after this week is over."

The kitchen is practical and beautiful with a large stone counter. It shimmers under the skylights above. The sink faces out over the courtyard, as do a row of stools and a dining table.

Jane spins around, clasping her hands in front of her chest as she smiles up at me. My heart thumps hard in my chest.

"I love this!" she exclaims.

She pauses, her brow furrowing as she looks up at me again. "Are we trapped in here?"

I chuckle. "Oh no, we can leave, but—" I smile down at her. "I think we might not want to. Food will be delivered, and we can order whatever we want."

"Will my phone from Earth even work here?"

I chuckle. "It will."

"Well, then what's for breakfast?" She approaches the refrigerator, swinging it wide open. It is completely stocked with options, including a fresh array of fruits and vegetables.

The morning passes quickly. We eat after I show her where the delivery area is, only to discover that a delivery has been made for us from our local bakery.

Jane wants coffee and worries that we won't have it.

"We have coffee. Humans have been coming to our planet for centuries, and we have our own drink that is similar," I explain. "A little less bitter, but stronger than caffeine."

She narrows her eyes, cocking her head to the side. "Is it a drug?"

I grin. "Well, technically, caffeine is a drug."

She rolls her eyes. After breakfast, I show her how to use her phone and get onto our version of a computer system here, which is much faster than what's available on Earth, then we go out into the courtyard. I hadn't even been allowed to tour this home until right before I went down to Earth, hoping to find a mate.

"It's beautiful," Jane says.

She turns slowly, her eyes arcing about the large inner courtyard. There's a small pond, and wild birds flit among the trees. She squeaks when she glances up. "There's a snake!" she yelps.

Its bright green iridescent scales shimmer under the sunlight. "They're harmless," I assure her.

Jane looks back toward me. "This is so weird."

"Weird?" I prompt as I step closer to her, unable to resist reaching for her hand.

She shrugs, looking a little sheepish. "Yes. I'm on another planet. And it's sort of like Earth, but way better. And you're here, and I'm a princess. I got married with a tiara," she marvels.

I chuckle, tugging her to me. "You *are* a princess here."

"Will everyone here call me princess all the time?" She angles her head to look up at me.

"Only in formal settings. Otherwise, you'll be Jane."

"And you'll be called Asher? Are you accustomed to being called prince?"

I shake my head. "I was crowned prince yesterday. Until then, I was just Asher."

She nods, falling quiet for a moment before adding, "I hope it works. I hope it stays good."

"What do you mean?"

She places her palm on my chest, and my heart feels as if it's lunging toward her touch. "This, with us," she clarifies.

"It will," I assure her.

"But how do you know?"

Releasing her hand, I slide my arm around her waist, cupping her cheek with my other palm as I bring her flush against me. My arousal is near instant.

"Don't you feel it?" I murmur, my voice low.

My hand slides down her neck over the wild beat of her pulse, and my thumb traces along her collarbone. I love the way her skin flushes pink so easily as if the desire rises to the surface swiftly in her.

"I do," she whispers, "but isn't that just lust?"

"Yes, but it's more than that. It's our infinity pulse."

I feel the rise of her breath and her breasts pressing against my chest. My cock throbs. Jane makes me crazy. I feel almost as if I'm a slave to her, bound so deeply already. It's as if she has lassoed my heart, the hold cinching tighter and tighter every time we touch.

"I feel it," she whispers.

She leans forward, and I feel her lips like a brand on my skin where she presses them to the divot at the base of my throat. She lifts her head, looking up at me. "Will living here change my skin?"

I shake my head. "Our children will probably have something between your skin and mine."

She bites her lip. My cock throbs again, and I feel my seed leaking out. It's been mere hours since I was buried deep in her, and I already need her again. I let my hand slip down over her bottom, bunching the fabric of her long skirt up in my fist to find she isn't even wearing panties.

"Oh, sweetheart," I groan. I give her bottom a squeeze.

She looks up at me, her eyes teasing. She reaches between us, dragging her palm boldly over the hard ridge of my arousal.

"You said we have a job this week," she murmurs throatily.

I tease my fingers between the cleft of her bottom, sliding my hand down to find her hot and slick. I growl into her hair. "Oh, Jane."

I glance around, and my eyes land on a bench in a corner. "This way," I bite out as I force myself to step back.

A moment later, we're in front of the bench, and she's bending over. I push her skirt up, baring her bottom. I nearly weep at the sight of her. She's so wet for me, quivering.

I tease my fingers between her thighs, sliding into her swollen folds and pumping deeply. I swiftly undo the laces on my breeches, and my cock springs free. My cum is sliding down my shaft.

As tempting as it is to bury myself inside her from behind right now, I want to see her face. She straightens and kicks her skirt to the side while I yank my breeches down. A moment later, we're both naked, the fresh air warm on our skin.

She orders me to sit.

I love her when she's bossy.

I do just as she says, watching when she kneels in front of me, her tongue circling her lips. She drags her thumb across the tip of my cock, just before she leans down and sucks me into her mouth. My head falls back as I cry out with a ragged groan. She sucks me in deeply, teasing me some more. She leans back, releasing me with a pop. "Do you like that?"

My chest heaves as I nod. "But I need to be inside you," I say.

Because I do. I want her pussy filled with my seed again. I want her plump and pregnant as soon as possible.

Jane rises, her breasts bouncing a little when she straddles me. I look deep into her eyes, my heart thudding in recognition of who she is to me and all we will be together.

She lowers her hips, and I guide myself to her entrance. I hold still for a moment as I feel the kiss of her arousal on my thick crown. "Now," I say, and she sinks down, sheathing me in her rippling core.

My release threatens already, like lightning about to strike. I hold on, clinging to my discipline, until I feel her body begin to quicken. I already know the sound of her torch song. She makes these breathy little gasps. I reach between us to find her swollen clit and savor her sharp cry. I can feel her arousal dripping down my cock and balls as my own release crashes through me.

She rests against me a moment later, and I hold her close. It feels as if I could just be like this with her forever. We don't move for a while, long enough that when she does shift, my cock twitches in response, thickening, and lengthening again inside her. She leans back to look at me.

"Again," she says.

I slip a hand down to where were joined. Her clit is poking out, pink and plump. "Only if you can come for me," I murmur.

As I tease over her, she trembles, clenching around me yet again. "Just one more, sweetheart."

She gives it to me, and the sound she makes is so sweet. I watch as she rises, sliding down over my cum-covered cock, the mixture of our arousal dripping down over my shaft. She pulls another release from me, and I watch as she bites her bottom lip and cries out.

Chapter Fifteen

JANE

The week flies by, and Asher and I never leave our house. We lounge in our private courtyard and christen every possible surface we can. I marvel that I'd worried about what we would do when his mother told me we would have a week alone together. Ha!

Though I blush to think of just how much time we spent in pure carnal pleasure, I'm amazed at how easy it is to be with him. We tell each other everything. I tell him all about my life on Earth, about losing my parents, about the betrayal, and about how I had no one left there. He tells me all about his life. Although the environment here is much better, it's not perfect. There are skirmishes between the cowboy leagues on this planet and the tragedy of the storm that led to so many women dying. I learn about the plants and animals here and more about my role.

I will be queen someday, but he assures me that won't be soon since his parents are healthy. We talk about my job running the matchmaking service. As the week comes to an end, my feelings are bittersweet.

One morning, after he has yet again teased me to

an intense climax and come inside me, I roll my head to the side, looking at him. He is ridiculously handsome with sharp, angled cheekbones and his perfect mouth, his eyes so startlingly blue as they meet mine. I've grown accustomed to the shimmery scaled surface of his skin.

"When will I know if I'm pregnant?" I ask.

Asher rolls onto his side, sliding his palm over my belly. His touch is possessive and soothing at once. "In a month. I believe you are," he says.

Helena schedules a meeting with me two days after Asher and I finish our honeymoon. I leave our home that morning after a hot encounter in the shower and a lingering kiss from Asher to walk to the main center of town. After our week together, Asher took me on a town tour.

I don't know what I expected, but this planet is more advanced than Earth. This town is modern. Many people walk, but some ride these things that are sort of like bicycles but much faster. They levitate.

Asher has told me I have one available, but I enjoy walking so far. The people and aliens I encounter here are friendly and welcoming. I'm savoring the warm weather and the clean air. I pass by the market area of town, which is bustling with fresh produce stands.

I'm spoiled with our courtyard because we have fruits and vegetables right there. Asher tells me I don't have to worry about shopping, that we are supplied by his assistants, but I tell him I want to shop because it's something I've never gotten to do. We've had several ventures into the market to peruse items.

I walk into the offices, passing through a large gateway into a lovely, lush garden and approaching another modern building. Asher assures me that it's nothing fancy for them. Even in the green zones on

Earth, there was nothing this fancy. Some buildings had once been nice, but they were mostly run-down now.

The door is held open for me by two people waiting outside. The queen is passing by in the main area. She's looking at something on a computer tablet. She glances up, pausing to smile at me. "Jane, good morning," she says.

I'm still nervous around her. She's so serene and beautiful and carries her authority with a comfortable warmth. "Hello, Alisha," I say.

"I understand Helena is meeting with you today?" she prompts with a lilt of a question in her voice.

I nod. "She wants to discuss the matchmaking service."

"We are looking forward to your plans."

No pressure. None at all. A freaking queen of another planet who happens to be my mother-in-law thinks I can handle this. Sure, sure.

Hopefully oblivious to my train of thought, she gestures for me to follow her. "Come with me for a moment."

I follow her, feeling so not very royal. We walk down a hallway and through a doorway into what must be Helena's office. A table sits to one side, and lush plants hang in the corner.

Helena stands quickly and curtsies. "My queen," she says.

Seriously.

Asher's mother angles her head to the side. "You needn't stand on ceremony, Helena."

Helena shrugs and winks. "It's fun." Her expression shifts to all business as she rubs her palms together. "Let's check in about the planning."

Alisha stays quiet as Helena gets started. As

Helena and I dive into the details, I realize this match-making service isn't simply about romance. It's not that I didn't grasp that when Asher explained how many women had perished in the storm that struck their planet, but I hadn't contemplated what that would mean for families and the survival of their species.

"There are far more men here now," Helena says. "This is a planetary problem for us."

"How many women are we talking?" I finally ask

Helena clasps her hands in front of her. "As many as are willing to come to our planet. We'd like to start with fifty for the leadership and then go from there after that."

"Fifty?" I squeak.

If she notices my surprise, Helena doesn't address it. She nods, her tone calm as she continues. "We're starting with the leadership and then on from there. Not everyone will experience infinity pulse like you and Asher. For some, it will be a practical choice."

"But it's been two years," Asher's mother interjects. "Our birthrate has dropped dramatically. It's not just that so many died in the storm. We also have to deal with the opposition leadership from Silver." I'm grateful Asher has given me a mini-geography lesson because I recall that's the other big city on this planet. "We are planning to meet with them and hopefully get them to understand how important this is for them and for our planet to stay strong."

They both look toward me expectantly. I take a breath. "So this is a big deal, and I have to find plenty of women to travel here. I understand and know we can do this," I say quickly. "Life on Earth is plain shitty for women. There's frequent violence, and we've lost so many rights. Ever since the environment got so bad, people are desperate."

"We understand," Alisha says. "We have a lot to offer here. Humans have traveled here for centuries because of our planet's similarity to Earth. I'm going to leave the logistics up to you and Helena. She will help you with the travel and so on, but you are our main leader on Earth for this mission, and you are our princess." I still can't even wrap my brain around *that* detail.

A buzzing sound happens, and Helena glances down at the tablet on the table. "I need to deal with the issue with the fountain. I'll be right back."

She hurries out. Alisha studies me for a moment, and I try not to get too anxious as I twist my hands together under the table. "You are pregnant. I have no doubt," she announces.

"You think so?" I squeak.

She nods. "How do you feel, and when is your cycle due?"

"I feel fine. My cycle is due in two weeks. We couldn't have known it, but the timing was very good for, um, well..." My cheeks get hot. "Our wedding."

Asher's mother nods along.

"What leads you to think I'm pregnant?"

"It's more of a feeling."

I place my hand over my belly, and it feels flat. "I won't know until I'm showing."

"You'll know sooner. Fertility is powerful for women from Earth here. We discovered that when travel among planets began happening."

"I want to be pregnant. I know it's important."

"It is, of course, but more than anything, I'm happy Asher found you. You are meant to be his princess."

The mere thought of Asher creates a sense of warmth in my chest around my heart. If you had told me I was going to move to another planet and fall in love with a space cowboy two weeks ago, I would've laughed so hard it hurt. Now, I can't imagine my life without Asher.

Alisha is called away just as Helena returns to her office. Helena and I continue planning and craft a new ad. She wants to do the royalty-in-space thing again. "How many princesses can there be?" I ask.

"Oh, just one. But we can focus on marrying into the leadership of the royal family. I've seen the news on Earth. Those old celebrity magazines are filled with news about the royals."

I ponder this, realizing that I probably wouldn't have clicked on the ad if it hadn't mentioned royalty. "Makes sense," I finally say. "How often will I be going to Earth?"

"We'll have to see how it goes. We're going to bring women here. The only reason Asher was there was because we had to start with him. He needed a mate, and he found you."

Again, warmth curls around my heart. "I feel so lucky," I say.

Helena studies me for a minute. "Asher is a good man. I knew the minute you walked in that you were the princess for him. I suppose with the situation on Earth that you do feel lucky. But you have a big responsibility now. It's important. I hope you're up for the challenge."

Anxiety churns inside, but I manage to nod. "I am. Maybe I've never done anything like this, but I'm ready."

Helena and I create several ads to spread far and wide on Earth. There are only a few online channels available. We review travel plans. She assures me I will never be going to Earth alone, that we'll always be on a ship. Once we get this coordinated and organized, it may even be possible for me to stay here and meet women as they arrive on this end.

We're just finishing up when there's a light knock on her door. "Yes?" she calls out.

Before the door even opens, I sense that it's Asher. This vibration happens when he's nearby, and I can't ignore it.

He steps into the room. Electricity sizzles through me with that now familiar heat spinning like fire in my veins.

His eyes meet mine. "I heard you were here and thought I'd stop by. Walk with me. I want to show you something if you're done here."

Helena stands and smiles at us. "She's all yours. We have a plan, and we're going to start next week. Are you going to come with us on the trips to Earth?" she asks.

"Whenever I can." He glances back at me. "Do not worry. It's completely safe. You will always go on our fastest ship."

"Okay," I say, feeling a little breathless. He has the craziest effect on me.

We depart, and Asher's hand clasps mine as we leave. He has told me that we will have protection throughout my pregnancy. Like his mother, he's convinced I'm already pregnant. He tells me so every night. Merely thinking about it makes me wet.

"What do you want to show me?" I ask, trying to stay focused.

He smiles down at me. I'm aware of the guards trailing us. I'm still getting accustomed to them constantly being nearby now that we're out of the protected realm of our home.

"Just a pretty walk," he says. "It's a favorite place of mine, and I want to share it with you."

We walk through the archway that leads out of the main government offices. A few moments later, we're in one of those hovering vehicles that zips us across the landscape and drops us off beside a shimmering lake.

"This is Lapis Loch. You showed it to me just the other day," I say.

He nods as he falls into step beside me. "I did, but I want to show you my favorite place."

He leads me through some silvery-blue trees down a path lined with stones. Everything feels hushed and quiet here. He turns down another path, and the guards fall back. He says to me, "This area is under protection."

He has explained to me before that there are areas that have special protection powers because they're important to his people.

We keep walking, and I try to stay focused. This ridiculous thing happens when I'm alone with Asher. I become wildly turned on. It's almost embarrassing. Here he is, trying to show me something important to him, and my panties are wet. I silently laugh to myself. To think that before I met Asher, I would've rolled my eyes so hard they almost fell out of my head if someone had told me that I would want any man this much.

He keeps leading me through the trees until the path turns again, and the view opens up. I realize we're on the opposite side of the lake now. I can see the town on the other side of the lake, rising up into the misty blue mountains. My breath catches in my throat.

"Oh, it's beautiful, Asher," I breathe.

He smiles down at me as I turn to look up at him. "It is."

There's a small bench here, and he catches my hand in his, tugging me with him as he sits down.

"Come closer," he says, bringing me between his knees. Our gazes are almost level. He's so tall, and I've come to love that I always feel sheltered and protected with him.

"How are you adjusting?" he asks, his thumb brushing along the side of my wrist, the touch utterly distracting as if licks of fire emanate from it.

"I love it here," I say fervently.

"Good."

He leans forward just slightly and slides his other hand around my waist, coaxing me forward. Seconds later, we're kissing, and I let myself tumble into it. Kissing him is always *so* very good. His tongue glides against mine, his mouth commanding and devouring at once.

Before I know it, I'm making these little whimpers in my throat and arching against him, almost frantic to get closer.

Asher murmurs, "Easy, love," against my lips.

But I'm too frantic. I need him. I need him inside me. We fumble, and I free him from his laced breeches and straddle him as he tugs my skirt up around my hips. His fingers tease into my dripping wet pussy.

"Oh, sweetheart. All for me," he growls.

I bite my lip and rock my hips over the hard ridge of his arousal. I rise up as he positions his cock at my entrance.

On the heels of a shuddering breath, I sink down over him. He controls my descent as I sheathe him.

This, just *this*, is exactly where I belong. Joined with the only man who is meant to be mine.

"Look at me," he rasps.

I open my eyes to find his gaze waiting. He rocks his hips, slowly nudging deeply each time. The friction from where we're joined sends piercing jolts of pleasure through me. I'm chasing my release, near desperate for it. Just when I think I can hardly bear it anymore, he reaches between us, and his fingers tease over my swollen clit. Pleasure crashes over me and through me. I'm shaking from the force of it.

I hear myself crying his name. He grips my hips tightly, thrusting upward, and I feel the heat of his release filling me.

We shudder together as I curl against him. He wraps his arms around me, holding me close.

My heartbeat echoes with the rhythm of his.

Chapter Sixteen

ASHER

This feeling with Jane warm in my arms, a soft bundle, is everything. Before I met her, I'd been told about the infinity pulse. It's not that I doubted it, but until I met her, I didn't realize how intense it would feel.

When we're joined like this, after we've both found our release with each other, it's all I ever want—this deep intimacy with her.

Long moments pass by, and she eventually lifts her head from where it's nuzzled into the curve of my shoulder. I open my eyes to find her smiling. She lets out a happy little sigh.

"Wow," she says. "It's always perfect."

"It is," I agree.

"Is this why you brought me here, to have your way with me again?" she teases.

I chuckle as I shake my head. "I just wanted to show you this place. But this makes it better."

A few minutes later, we put our clothes back into place and walk back.

"I have to go back to meet with the leadership and discuss various issues," I explain when we've returned to Jane's designated office in the main building. "You'll be busy."

"I know." She nods. "It feels very official."

"You are our princess now."

Her shoulders rise with a breath. "I'm nervous to go back to Earth."

"I'll do the first several trips with you. I promise. Once it's up and running, you'll be completely in charge. I'm just there to keep you company, really."

"Okay, I'm nervous, but I can handle it."

I lean down, giving her a quick and fierce kiss. "I have complete faith in you."

"What are you meeting about?" she asks.

"We're working on dealing with the unrest with the other city. Don't worry, it's fine. We're married, and you're pregnant. They can no longer challenge the order of succession."

She gives me a cheeky grin. "You're a little optimistic about me being pregnant."

I wink. "I am, but I also believe it."

I leave her there just as Helena approaches the hallway to meet her again. Moments later, I am in my office with my father and Kayden, my closest friend and leader of the royal guard.

"What's the problem now?" I ask.

"Honnell and his minions are grumbling, a lot, about our plan. Yet they don't dispute that Jane is your princess. We're going to have to keep negotiating to keep things quiet. On the one hand, they are yammering on about purity and not relying on finding mates from Earth. On the other, they want dibs on all available women in our area. We aren't going to subject women to their ridiculous ideas."

"They might as well go to Earth," I deadpan. "That's how women are treated there."

"I suggested the same," my father says dryly.

I glance around, my gaze arcing over the landscape outside the windows. It's beautiful here. I love my planet, and I want to protect my people. If only those who call themselves pure understood the realities that we face. We are stronger when we connect with others.

The people from Earth are part of our history. We are descended from the same planet before our kind spread across the galaxy.

I look back toward Kayden and then my father. "We will fight, if we must. Until then, let's hope the peace holds."

Kayden departs a moment later, and I check with my father. He has always been all-powerful to me yet benevolent. He has chosen a truce with the other side of the planet, which I respect. It makes sense. Although, at times, I have wondered if we need to act with more force.

He turns from the windows to face me. He studies me for a moment as his lips curl slowly into a smile. "I am happy for you and Jane. You finally found your mate."

It feels as if my heart smiles when I think of Jane. "I did. We leave tomorrow for Earth. She will begin the matchmaking service. She and Helena will manage it."

"You're going with her?" he prompts.

"Yes. At first."

"She will be safe without you, of course."

I take a breath. "I know, but..." I shrug.

"You do not want to be without her. That is when you know it's a true match," my father says.

"Are you concerned about Honnell?" I ask.

My father nods as his gaze sobers. "This is an

endless and pointless conflict. We have always been stronger as a species by mating with humans from Earth. It is, after all, our sister planet. Yet they don't see that and refuse to learn from history. When I step down, you will continue to face this problem and just have to keep doing what you must do. The need is even more important now. Ever since the storm."

"I know. Hopefully, once we start this process, it will help," I say.

I depart the office a few minutes later to find Kayden waiting outside. He grins as he waggles his brows. He was present at my wedding, but today is the first day I've seen him since because he was traveling while I was enjoying my week with Jane. We haven't had a chance to speak about anything but business yet.

"I see you survived your honeymoon," he offers with a wink.

I chuckle. "I certainly did."

"You must be exhausted," he teases, cuffing me lightly on the shoulder.

I roll my eyes. "I am stronger than ever."

He cocks his head to the side. "Jane is stunning. Just tell me when the matchmaking service starts. I'm going to offer myself up as the next test case."

"You can come with us tomorrow. We're going to Earth."

"I'll be there."

"We will recruit women to bring them here. Here's hoping it goes well."

"Well, if you and Jane are any indication, it shall," he says. "See you tomorrow."

"Sunrise!" I call as I turn and continue walking out.

This afternoon, I will introduce Jane to her mount. We ride horse-like creatures here with sharp tails.

While I love the thrill of a ride, what I want now is

Jane. My pulse quickens at the mere thought of her. I'm still adjusting to the intensity of my emotions for her. The feelings extend far beyond want and need.

She commands me on every level, and I will do anything to protect her and protect and cherish what we have.

Chapter Seventeen

JANE

"Um, you want me to what?" I squeak as I look up at Asher.

Until right this second, things have been going swimmingly. Sexy space cowboy alien sweeps me off my feet to a new planet where I can leave my craptastic life in the dust. Everything seems fabulous so far until Asher tells me it's time to meet my horse. The closest earthly creature I can compare it to is maybe a seahorse combined with a dragon and a horse with a sharp tail that looks downright scary.

The horse stares at me, his dark coat shimmering with glints of deep blue. Asher looks down at me, and I see the glimmer of humor entering his gaze. "Have you ever ridden a horse on Earth?"

"No!" I exclaim and lift one of my feet. "I could get anywhere I needed to go walking. I didn't have far to go. Plus, you know there aren't many horses left there," I point out. "Do I have to do this?" I'm hedging, and I know it, but my eyes land on the horse's tail again. It's not flowing and made of hair, but thin with a barbed tip, sort of like what I imagined a dragon would have. "Are you sure this isn't a dragon?"

My husband shakes his head. "It's a type of horse." He studies me for a moment. "You are our princess and need to be able to ride. It's not something you have to do often, but it will seem as though you're not fully one of us if you don't."

I wrinkle my nose, resting my hands on my hips. "Fine. Let's do it, then."

A few minutes later, after he has explained the process to me, Asher has his hands on my waist to lift me into the saddle. Once again, I'm distracted. He has this wildly inconvenient effect on me where I can't think straight if he touches me. My pulse riots, and my belly does a little shimmy. Meanwhile, he's all helpful.

"I'm going to lift you," he says.

"Okay," I chirp.

He lifts me easily, reminding me how strong he is. Next thing I know, I'm sitting atop this land seahorse-dragon. "He sure is pretty," I say, admiring his shimmering coat. "Now what?" I ask.

I glance over my shoulder to see Asher walking over to his horse and quickly climbing on it. "Stay with me," he says, appearing to talk to my horse.

"You forgot to tell me his name," I call as Asher begins moving with my horse following.

"Lazuli," he calls over his shoulder.

It feels like I'm sitting in a rocking chair at first, but then Lazuli starts moving much faster than I want. There's nothing for me to hold on to, not even any reins. "What the hell?" I mutter to myself. Lazuli comes to a quick stop, and I steady myself as the horse turns to glance at me. I could swear this horse-alien-dragon understands what I'm saying.

"I've never ridden anything like this," I say apologetically.

Lazuli looks away, actually sighing. This is my life —an alien horse sighs at me.

He begins walking at a sedate pace. Asher circles, looking kind of hot and sexy as he approaches. "That's all there is to it. How do you feel?"

Lazuli simply keeps walking as I shrug. "Fine? I think. I'm not ready to go any faster."

"No need," Asher returns with a grin.

"Is it like the wave?" I ask a few minutes later after we have returned the horses to their field.

"The wave?" Asher looks genuinely confused and puzzled.

"On Earth, they call it the beauty queen wave where you practice your hand thing?" I demonstrate. "For when they're in parades," I clarify. "Not that there's been a parade in my entire life on Earth, but I read about them in school."

Asher chuckles. "Sure. We don't have any parades, but I understand what you mean. Are you ready for tomorrow?" he asks.

"I think that'll be easier than this," I offer with a saucy grin. We're walking back to our house, and I can't wait to get home.

I know there are plenty of other things to do with my life here, but I wouldn't mind spending all my time with Asher alone.

Chapter Eighteen

JANE

I didn't realize how nervous I was on my trip from Earth to here until we got back on the same ship to return to Earth. I'd been too anxious to absorb much on my initial journey. Now, I have a gazillion questions about the spaceship and all kinds of things. Asher answers every question I have, and his friend Kayden is bemused by us.

Meanwhile, Helena is busy checking applications for the job. We have hundreds of applicants, which doesn't surprise me one bit.

I tell her to go ahead and approve them all. I shrug. "We'll see who shows up. It'll be like a job fair."

Her eyes go wide. "We need women. I've looked around, and there are legit not many women on your planet," I point out.

"*Our* planet," Asher interjects with a wink.

"Kayden is our test case," I say with a wave toward him.

He chuckles while Asher adds, "I'm the test case."

"Not anymore. We're married."

His return grin is sly, and my belly shimmies. I

keep thinking this wild, rampaging desire for him will calm the hell down. But my hormones are just out of control when it comes to Asher. Which I suppose is handy. I think I'm pregnant because my body feels subtly different.

Before I know it, we're on Earth. "That only took us two hours." I glance toward Asher. "Is this how long it takes normally?"

"It depends. Cargo trips take longer."

"You're royalty," Kayden chimes in. "You get the fast flight."

It's strange to walk out of the ship, excuse me, spaceship, and get struck by the blast of dry heat here on Earth. Until a few weeks ago, this weather was all I'd known. The contrast to Aphroditea's fresh air is stark.

A haze of smoke in the air lets me know the wildfires are burning up North. There have been wildfires burning for years on Earth, my entire life and then some. The history books tell us it wasn't always that way, but it has been for me. There isn't much left to burn, but the fires still catch and burn through dry brush and scrub in areas. Smoke follows. The smoke is pushed around by the wind, swirling in dusty eddies.

The smoke isn't too bad today. I look up at Asher, asking, "Do you bring masks when you come to Earth in case the smoke is bad?"

He nods. "We have them and breathing gear if needed. It doesn't seem that bad today."

"It's not," I offer, well aware it could be so smoky that we couldn't even see.

Things move at a brisk pace once we've arrived. Asher and his bodyguards depart for a meeting somewhere. Helena brings me to the office where I met Asher for the first time.

"We own this building," she explains as we walk down the hallway.

"The whole building?"

She nods. "Yes. We have many applicants. We've never had a job fair on our planet, but I've read they have them on Earth all the time."

"Jobs are hard to come by. Everyone's a little desperate for a halfway-decent life. And if they're anything like me, they want a chance to leave Earth. Only the very wealthy can afford it. The rest of us hope we can land a place to live in the green zone." I pause to glance out the windows. There isn't a speck of green visible. "Maybe someday Earth will rebound enough to be the way it was before."

Helena shrugs. "Maybe. That's a long way off. They need more resources to make that possible."

I have so many questions. I want to understand this relationship with my new people and those who are on Earth. I knew we traveled to other planets, but I didn't know aliens and humans mated. I'm curious about the galaxy beyond as well. In my first few weeks on my new planet, I've been so caught up in Asher and the wonder of being somewhere beautiful and safe that I haven't had time to focus on much else.

I've gleaned that there's a lot of intergalactic travel, and it's fairly common. Earth seems to be behind the ball, from what I can piece together. Today isn't the day for those questions. Helena and I get organized quickly. There's a downstairs area with a larger room. I realize this building must've once been a school because it's an old gymnasium.

In short order, Helena and I are screening applicants. I find myself protective of the men on Aphroditea. I screen out several applicants right off the bat because they seem too shallow. I feel twinges of guilt for even thinking like that. I, too, had been desperate before.

Helena tells me it's important to remember we want to give these women a better life. Life on Earth is abysmal. Women are often abused and practically secondhand citizens. They need to be brave simply to survive.

About halfway through, I find the first woman I think should definitely be a candidate. She's pretty with bouncy honey-gold curls and freckled cheeks. Her name is Nadine. Our interview process is fairly simple. We discuss the planetary differences and the expectations for a woman on our planet. At first, it sounded strange to call it our planet, but Helena repeatedly reminded me that I was one of the leaders there now and that I was a true princess.

Pain flashes in Nadine's eyes when I ask her what prompted her to apply. "I'm just going to be honest," she finally says, her voice low. "I was about to marry into a family in the green zone, a wealthy family. But I couldn't do it because he was abusive."

She swallows audibly after she takes an unsteady breath. It's only then that I notice she's used makeup to cover a bruise underneath one of her eyes. My heart gives a painful thump, and a familiar sense of anxiety races through me. Even though I managed to avoid being beaten, it's common here.

"So I left, and now I'm desperate because I have nothing, and I'm afraid."

My belly clenches with worry. "When did you leave?"

She blinks back tears. "This morning."

The murmur of voices carries on around us. The room is filled with a line of applicants. Along with Helena, another woman helps us with interviews.

Just then, the back door to the large room opens, and Asher enters. I don't even have to look that way to know it's him because that vibration, which is still startling but becoming familiar to me, starts humming in my body. The sensation becomes stronger until he stops beside me and places a hand on my shoulder.

I smile up at him. "Hello," I murmur.

His reply is a kiss. He bends low to dust one on my cheek. The touch of his lips sends a fiery sizzle of electricity through me. As he straightens, I gesture toward Nadine. "This is Nadine. I've already decided she'll be coming back with us today."

Asher smiles warmly at her as he nods. Just then, the door opens again and Kayden comes through, immediately walking in our direction once he spies Asher.

Nadine fidgets in her seat nervously. Asher looks from her toward Kayden. "You will marry him," he says with complete confidence.

"I will?!" she squeaks.

Before Asher can reply, Kayden reaches us and stops beside him. Asher and I might as well be invisible. Kayden's gaze is locked on Nadine.

Kayden finally looks toward Asher and me. He holds his hand out to Nadine as she looks at me uncertainly. "I need to talk with her privately," he announces.

When Asher catches my eyes and nods, I reply, "Go ahead."

Kayden takes Nadine's hand, and they leave through the back of the room. "Will they marry now?" I whisper to Asher.

He shakes his head. "Not until we get back to our planet."

I've been focused solely on finding mates, so I

didn't think beyond the initial phase. "So it's impor-tant for everyone to marry *on* the planet?"

"They must. It's binding."

"Oh, well, that's good to know," I tease.

He winks, and my pulse kicks up its pace.

"How is this going?" he asks.

It's so silly, but these moments when we're just talking seem mundane, but his attention is so focused on me I could practically swoon.

"Good, I think," I say, forcing my attention away from him and glancing around the room quickly. We have selected five candidates so far. "Helena wants to leave today with five candidates or more."

"Good." He paused, and I feel the warmth of his palm sliding over my shoulder. "I'm ready to go," he says.

"Asher," I whisper after he leans down again and gives me a lingering kiss, even teasing his tongue against mine.

"Yes, my love?" he murmurs.

I feel the clench of my pussy. I can't even reply.

"I can't wait to get back to our planet. We need to go home, and I need to be inside you."

I've never had anyone speak to me as bluntly as Asher does. It's direct and naughty, yet it feels like another form of love with him, so dirty and intimate. I feel like the slick moisture between my thighs.

He glances at Helena. "Can I speak privately with my princess?" he asks.

"Of course," she replies.

He leads me quickly out of the room, down the hallway, and up to the office we met in before. My eyes land on the nondescript plastic table.

In a burning second, Asher is kissing me. My entire body is aflame with need as he takes deep sips from my mouth. He closes the door behind us, and I hear the snick of the lock. Pressing me to the door, he slides his hand down to catch the hem of my skirt and drags it up.

At his request, I go bare with nothing underneath. I never know when he may need me or I may need him. His fingers delve into my slippery-wet and swollen folds.

"Oh, love," he growls against my mouth as his fingers tease into me, pumping once and then again.

"Asher..." I whimper as he lifts his head. I'm on fire for him, just him.

He palms my cheek with one hand, and he slides it down to drag his thumb across my kiss-swollen lips. I can't help it, and my tongue darts out to taste his skin. I savor the salty tang.

His eyes darken. "I love you, Jane," he murmurs.

"And I love you," I return just as he pumps his fingers into me again, and my pussy squeezes around them. "I need you," I rasp.

He spins us around, moving quickly across the room and sliding my hips onto the table. My skirt is bunched up around my hips. He pushes my knees apart, his eyes dropping down. I can literally feel the heat of his stare between my thighs.

He kneels in front of me, and it truly feels as if he is worshipping me as his palms slide down my thighs. His touch is strong and sure.

"Look," he says.

I follow his gaze down to my pussy. Watching his fingers slide through my slippery arousal is beyond filthy, and I am so needy. "Asher," I beg.

Chapter Nineteen

ASHER

I'm dancing along the edge of pain. My cock is so hard that I can feel cum leaking out the tip as it swells to press against the laces of my breeches. I lift my eyes to see Jane looking down just as I've asked her to do.

I tease my fingers into her glistening pink folds, sliding two in at once. She bites her lips as she whimpers, and her pussy tightens in a rippling clench around my fingers.

Her clit is pink and plump, pushing out. "Soon, you will be round with my baby. Look at your needy little clit," I say as I circle my thumb over it.

She cries out sharply, and I feel the pulse of her heartbeat in her clit. My own cock is beating with need.

"Please, Asher," she rasps.

I pump my fingers into her again. As much as I want to make her come right now, I need to be inside her when it happens. I straighten, ordering her, "Turn around and bend over."

Jane, my princess, moves with alacrity. She shimmies off the table and spins around, bending over to show me her beautiful bottom, her curves generous. I'm yanking at the laces on my breeches, and my cock springs free, cum rolling down its length.

"Hurry," she begs, pushing her hips back to meet me as I bring my thick crown to her entrance.

On the heels of a breath, I fill her swiftly. She cries out, and I feel her arousal building. I reach around to tease my fingers over that needy clit of hers, letting out a growl of satisfaction when I feel her coming as she cries my name. She shudders all over and pushes her hips back into me, taking all of me into her silky, clenching sheath.

My release is fierce, like a clap of thunder in my body. Once more, I pour my seed into her. I know she's already pregnant, but something about knowing that she'll be walking around with my seed wet between her bare thighs is so primal.

I smooth a palm up her spine, needing the connection. I let it rest between her shoulder blades, where I can feel the beat of her heart. Her soft sigh spins around my heart like a little lasso, cinching tight. She may be mine, but more than that, I am hers. She *owns* my heart.

We disentangle ourselves and tidy our clothes. A few moments later, she turns to look up at me, her cheeks stained pink. She looks almost bashful. I love this about her. She's wild and free when we're intimate. In the aftermath, she's always a touch shy about it.

I step closer again, lifting a hand to brush a loose lock of hair off her cheek. "What is it, love?" I ask, my voice low as I search her eyes.

She bites her lip before she takes a quick breath. "*You.* Obviously, I never expected to be a princess on another planet. And I certainly never imagined I could feel like this with someone."

She places her palm over my heart, and it lunges toward her touch, recognizing its owner.

I never expected a woman from Earth to be my princess. And even though I knew of infinity pulse, its power is more than I expected. I place my palm over the back of her hand, holding her gaze as I take a steadying breath. "You are everything to me. I'm so glad I found you."

I'm leaning to kiss her when there's a sharp knock on the door. Helena's voice reaches us. "I'm sure you're busy, but we're here for business," she calls.

Jane bites her lip as she giggles. I lower our clasped hands, and we walk toward the door together. I watch over the next few hours as Jane deftly handles the crush of applicants.

Maybe we didn't quite catch that the concept of royalty on Earth is more of a news thing than anything, but as Jane pointed out, it's a draw. There's that, and the fact that life on earth isn't great. For anyone, but even more so for women.

By the end of the day, they've selected four women to return to the planet. One of them is already bonded to Kayden, although I wonder if he will believe in the power of infinity pulse. My old friend and lead body-guard is cynical.

I reach for Jane's hand as we walk back toward the spaceship. She smiles up at me as her fingers lace with mine. "You handled that perfectly, my princess," I murmur.

Her eyes twinkle. "You think?"

"Yes, I can already tell those you've selected will handle the transition to a new planet well."

"I hope I don't work myself out of a job," she teases.

I shake my head. "You won't. And if you do, there will be something else."

We reach the ship, and it's all business as we get on board.

Chapter Twenty

JANE

I've already told Helena and Asher that it's important for the women coming with us to get a debriefing on the ship so they can be prepared when we land on Aphroditea. Helena has arranged for a conference room on the ship to be made available. It's very utilitarian, like the whole ship.

Helene leaves me with the four women, gesturing toward me before she departs. "This is Princess Jane. She will help you prepare for what happens next."

I smile around the women. We've selected Nadine, Anna, Beth, and Emma. Even if she doesn't fully grasp what it means, Nadine is already matched. I recognize the look in her eyes. They are wide and swirling with a combination of anticipation and uncertainty.

So are the others, but they have yet to experience that feeling of meeting their mate. I can't even believe how experienced I feel. I've only been on my new planet for a few weeks. Even if it's still all fresh and almost shocking, I do understand what it must be like for them.

I look among them. "How do you feel?" I begin.

One of the women clasps her hands together, her thumbs twisting nervously as she looks among the group. "Overwhelmed. I can't believe I did this. When I saw the ad, I thought it had to be a scam."

"I thought it was a joke when I saw it," I agree. "I applied anyway because Earth is dry and hot."

"And the women are treated like shit," another woman chimes in bluntly.

"We have very few opportunities there. I promise you Aphroditea is much better for us. They revere women there," I add.

Nadine glances from me to the other women. "So, um, what was that thing with your husband when he said I would marry?"

"He believes you are experiencing a infinity pulse with Kayden. It's intense, isn't it?" I prompt.

She takes a deep breath, letting it out in a shuddery sigh. "Yes. But he didn't say we would marry."

"Give it time," I offer encouragingly. Asher had seemed confident about it, but I'm still getting to know Kayden.

"What's the planet like?" another woman asks.

"I imagine it's a bit like Earth used to be. There are mountains and lakes and sunshine and rain. The sun there is not as hot and bright as Earth's sun."

Another woman asks, "What if we don't mate with someone?"

"I'm confident you will."

Nadine drums her fingertips on the table. "Why do they need women there?"

"Every year, they have a festival in honor of women. Two years ago, a large space storm during the festival killed many women. As a result, far more men than women now inhabit the planet. It's a concern because they need women for families. They have mated with humans for centuries. Asher and his kind are all descended from cowboys who traveled there from Earth several centuries ago. They have evolved since then. They're taller and stronger, and their skin is scaled and bronzed. Genetically, they can mate with humans. It makes the offspring stronger than either species individually."

"Oh, well, that makes sense," Nadine replies.

"So we're not just going to be there by ourselves if we don't meet someone fast," Anna prompts.

"Of course not. You'll be staying together so you don't feel alone. The planet's environment is much better than Earth's. You'll be safe," I assure them.

The women pepper me with other questions. I answer as many questions as I can and ask Helena and her assistant for more information. It's not too long before we land on the planet.

I'm surprised to feel a sense of relief inside. It's amazing to me how quickly this place has come to feel like home. I'm excited to be here and feel safe with Asher again.

Chapter Twenty-One

ASHER

Jane glances over at me. "Wow," she says.

It's only been two days, and the crush of men jostling to meet the women from Earth has been overwhelming. "I don't want to put them on display," she adds.

"Of course not," I agree.

Given how many women died during the storm, the interest doesn't surprise me. What surprised me was how many were coming from the other side of our planet. As my parents have said for years, Honnell's leadership is out of touch with their people.

"How often do you think I need to go down to Earth? I was thinking once a month would be enough," Jane comments.

I study her for a moment. "It's your decision."

"It is?"

"Absolutely," I say firmly. "You are in charge. You're my princess. No one here doubts your authority in these matters."

"But I want your opinion," she presses.

"I think once a month will be a good start. I think

maybe you alternate between bringing women here and bringing men there. We love to travel."

"But Earth is —"

"Hot and dry," I interject. "Traveling to other planets only makes me appreciate ours so much more. Unlike Earth, we don't limit our people from information about other planets. We're not the only nice planet around."

When she smiles up at me, my heart thumps hard. She doesn't have to do much to elicit my body's reaction. She's my mate and always will be. "That's why you're called space cowboys," she teases.

I chuckle. "We will mostly stay on our planet here because of our responsibilities to our people. When you feel more settled, and after you've had our baby, we should travel some together. You can see other planets."

Her lips curl. "That would be nice. *If* I'm pregnant." She is more cautious than me in this matter. "I'll know soon."

"I already know."

Her cheeks flare with heat.

Later that evening, we have dinner in our courtyard. I'm surprised to discover that I always want more time with Jane. It's not that I doubt my feelings for her, but I had wondered if I'd be consumed with my work once our marriage and week of pleasure were over. Instead, she's always feathering along the edge of my thoughts. I want to savor more time with her uninterrupted and away from the demands of helping to lead our planet.

After dinner, I drizzle a sweet honey over her body. I lick her clean before once again filling her again and savoring the way she clenches around me, loving every sound she makes. I carry her to bed, and she curls up soft and warm by my side. This couldn't have turned out more perfectly. I've found her, the only woman for me.

I've already become accustomed to her patterns. I know at some point to she will wake in the darkness to go to the bathroom. I come awake and blink in and out of sleep when I feel her roll away from me and slip out of bed.

I don't know how much time has passed when I hear a muffled scream. I sit up swiftly to discover Jane still hasn't returned to bed with me.

I scramble out of bed, wrapping the sheet around my waist as I bolt out of the room. When I make it to the living room, I look up to discover the skylight is broken.

Anger and fear course through me. My parents had worried that Honnell and his men would try to inter-fere when I found a mate. The power struggle between my parents' generation was settled when my father took on the biggest threat to his crown. There'd been a few skirmishes, but my father had turned public sentiment against them after they threatened some women in our city.

Ever since I reached the age where it was time for me to find a mate, there have been jostling among the other league and calls for the royal leadership to change. I didn't care about the power so much, yet I did care about Honnell's men trying to take over. All they wanted was power. The situation on that side of our planet has been unstable ever since Honnell rose to power. They try to limit resources, though there's no need to whatsoever.

I have faith that Jane is already pregnant, and I know there can be no threats to our union. Yet now I must find her. Aware I can't get to her instantly, I grab my clothes and tap the communicator embedded into my shirt. "They've taken Jane!"

Kayden responds instantly. "We're already aware. I was just calling you."

"Fuck," I mutter under my breath. I shouldn't have been without my communicator, but I didn't expect anyone to target our home. The one weakness in our house is through the skylight.

If they transport to the roof undetected, that creates a safety issue even though we have a shield.

"What happened to the shield?" I ask as I reach for my weapons.

"They breached it on the side of the city, undetected. It was only as they were coming back through that we realized what happened," he replies. "I'm already on my way to you. We're tracing them."

This will be a quick fight, and I know we'll win. But I don't want Jane to be harmed, and I don't want her to be afraid. I have fought many battles. During the unrest for months after the storm, we had to fight off their attempts to take over power multiple times.

My fear for Jane and for her safety runs deep, and my anger is a ball of cold fire inside.

Within minutes, Kayden meets me out front. I'm communicating with my father as we leave. "We are leaving to get her now."

"Let me handle it," he replies, his tone brooking no argument.

I know why he's trying to insist on that. He wants to protect me, to protect our new union because we're the next generation of leadership.

But this is Jane, *my* princess. I cannot stay out of the fray. "Father, you can help, but I cannot stand back for Jane."

I hear my father's sharp inhalation. "Understood," he replies. "We will meet you at the ship."

In minutes, we have rendezvoused on the outer side of my home. The house I share with Jane is on the same property protected for our entire family. My parents live in another home nearby.

I glanced between Kayden and my father. "Who else shall we bring?"

"We have already sent out two teams ahead. They won't be able to keep her. Do not worry," my father says firmly.

Our local ships are much smaller than what we use to travel off the planet. They move swiftly.

Moments later, we are all on board. The pilot speeds across the planet until we hover over Silver, a town on the other side of the planet. This league descends from the French gardians, cowboys like us. Over time, we have had alliances that have ruptured and repaired. The latest leaders are restless after the storm. They did not choose to go to Earth and mate with more humans. They claim to be purists. I snort to myself as I consider the silly concept. Our species has intermingled with humans for centuries, strengthening our health mutually over the years.

That is why they keep fighting for power, for an alleged purity. We heard about it from Earth as well. That was part of the rupture for their people when the planet began to heat and some refused to make the choices necessary to take care of each other. On multiple planets in history, time and again, the cycles repeat. Some choose to expand and strengthen, whereas others try to build walls and weaken.

Our pilot hovers above, and I see two other ships in the sky above the shield for the city. It's technologically weaker than ours. Despite the challenges on

Earth, they have excellent technology and have protected their scientists for centuries. We have benefited from their knowledge, and they have benefited from ours.

While this current generation of gardians has closed out any new information and is relying on older technology.

"Find the weak spots," I say.

My heart pounds, and my entire being aches for Jane.

"Through!" my father calls as we dive in formation to break through their shields.

It is quiet once we can see the town more clearly. I realize what they want. They want us to be vulnerable, to have to fight on their turf. I will do whatever is necessary to bring Jane back and know we can win.

We land, and my father looks over at me. "I want you to wait here," he says.

Jane is afraid; I know she is. "I cannot allow Jane to be rescued by someone other than me."

My father's nostrils flare as he takes a breath, letting it out swiftly. I glance around as a team of elite soldiers steps out with us. It isn't just men. Our women are just as strong and powerful.

My mother's chin lifts as she approaches us. She is leading an elite team of young women trained to fight. "We will find Jane. That is how it will be," my mother tells me.

I study her for a beat before replying, "I will go with you."

My mother stares at me and dips her chin. A moment later, we are off, moving quickly through the darkness. I know this town and its landscape well. I have to. We were all of this planet. We slip through a copse of silvery trees. Our silver-gold moon lights the way.

Jane is the very beat of my heart. I want her safe. I want her back in my arms. The men who did this will pay.

Because of our infinity pulse, I know when we're getting close to where she's being held. I can feel her. The vibration echoes in my body. I lift a hand in the air, staying silent. We all stop.

I glance at my mother. "She's there." I point through the trees at a small square building in a ravine.

I hear it before we see them, but suddenly a group of soldiers is coming out to fight. My mother's team of soldiers is ruthless. We don't kill, though. Ever.

A blade drags down the side of my arm, yet my armor protects me. I ignore it, spinning to take down the man fighting. Moments later, we have them all subdued. My mother's soldiers are binding their hands with our vibrating ropes and ties. Their leader, Honnell, wrestles against his hold, ashamed to be brought down by our female fighters. I don't even bother to ask where Jane is being held. I keep following the vibration.

I leave my mother to interrogate him, while Kayden and others approach the small home with me. We dispatch the two guards swiftly. My heart aches as we walk into the building.

Jane stands from a wooden chair. Her eyes lock with mine, fear shimmering there.

"Asher!" she cries out.

From behind, another man steps forward, sliding his arm around her and lifting his gun to point directly at her neck. "If you take her, I will kill her," he says calmly.

Chapter Twenty-Two

JANE

It feels like forever since I've seen Asher. I knew he was coming to save me. I knew he was approaching because I could feel him. The vibration of our infinity pulse thrums with more force when he's near.

I hadn't realized how it would feel when we were apart. It feels as if my body has a sensor just for him. Asher holds my gaze. He says nothing, but I can feel his reassurance from across the room.

He is surrounded by soldiers, including Kayden. I recognize some of the faces of the women. In their gear, they look fierce.

"You will not win this," Asher says to the man holding me, his tone level. "You have no backup. If you kill our princess, you will lose your only bargaining chip."

The man, whose name I don't know, shuffles his feet. These men all seem angry and disorganized, a sense of reckless chaos driving them.

Ever since two men had broken through the skylight in our home and taken me, they'd been arguing. They bickered with each other on the small ship that flew us to this side of the planet. It's been one argument after another, all of them petty. I may not understand what they hope to gain, but it's clear they are not a unified group.

"We want a change in leadership, a new vote," the man says.

"There's a vote every year. You can't force a vote by kidnapping my princess and threatening to kill her," Asher states flatly.

I don't look away from Asher. His presence eases the fear churning inside me. I hold perfectly still. Because I have faith he can save me. I shift my hands slightly where they're tied behind my back. I had loosened the ties only moments ago when I felt Asher approaching. With the man holding me focused on Asher, I keep twisting them.

I feel one of the women's eyes on me. I carefully shift my eyes in her direction, and she nods, just barely. My heart pounds as I twist my wrists again, feeling the binding loosen. Another moment later, I manage to get the tie undone, catching the binding with my fingertips just before it falls to the floor.

My heart beats so hard my ribs hurt from the force of it. With anxiety churning in my gut, I summon my courage. The man is saying something to Asher, and I move swiftly, swinging my arm out and knocking the weapon from his hands. Everything is a blur. There is a shout from that man, and more burst forward from a darkened doorway in the corner.

Asher spins quickly, taking two of them down with some weapon. The soldiers with him quickly subdue the men who took me here.

One of them is arguing loudly, and Asher replies, "We've already taken them, you idiot. All of you will stand trial. Where is your shame for your community?

Your people are hungry, and you are taking unnecessary resources from them. They will say there is no point to this, yet you will still be stupid because you're jealous and power-hungry."

Only after Asher finishes speaking does he wrap both arms around me, holding me close. He cups the back of my head with one hand, while the other moves up and down my back in soothing passes.

I'm shaking with the fear, and tears sting my eyes as I breathe him in. I tuck my head into the curve of his shoulder, my fear dissipating with the feel of his heart beating.

"I have you," he whispers just above my ear. "We have to go."

I lift my head to meet his eyes. "I know. I love you," I say just before he kisses me fiercely.

In seconds, we are moving as the team with Asher closes ranks around us. Kayden barks out orders. We're outside in the darkness, where the cool air feels good against my skin. The queen is there, waiting for me, it seems.

"You are safe," she says, her hand sliding over my shoulder as we fall into step beside her. Asher has my hand in his. Everything is a jumble and a rush. Asher briefly confers with his parents and other leaders. Some of us will be leaving, and others will be staying behind to stand guard over those who kidnapped me. I hear discussion of a trial for those involved.

My heart feels like a bird trapped in my chest, beating so hard that the rushing sound of blood in my ears is overwhelming. Asher is holding me close, and I burrow into him, seeking his warmth and strength.

I'm trembling, and I don't realize I'm crying until I feel his palm moving in a slow circle between my shoulder blades. "You're safe."

I lift my face to meet his worried gaze. He brings his palm to my cheek, his thumb swiping my tears away. "You're safe," he repeats.

My heartbeat finally starts to slow from the wild galloping pace in my chest. I can see the anger swirling in his eyes. He's barely keeping his anger in check—not at me but at what happened.

"I'm okay," I say. "I don't think they meant to hurt me. They wanted to keep me until I had our baby."

"I know. And for that, they will pay," he says, his voice low.

"What do you mean?"

"We will have a trial. It will be public."

"Will they die?" My eyes go wide.

Earth has death sentences. "We don't do that here. We are civilized, fair, and just." Asher pauses, his eyes narrowing. "I fear those who carried out the kidnapping aren't the ones behind the planning."

I blink up at him. "I know. What happens now?"

"Tonight, you and I are going home. We've already repaired the breach in the city shields and above our house. My father has called up our reinforcements for patrol. For now, we must go."

Once again, things happen swiftly as wc rush to get to the ship. Another ship lands just as we're leaving. Asher's mother orders the arriving crew to take the prisoners back.

I can't stop touching Asher. I need to be physically linked with him at all times. I was never afraid for my life, except at the very beginning. Yet I was so afraid I would somehow not get back to him. I feared for our baby. While I still don't know with certainty that I'm pregnant, I feel like I am. I won't know until I miss my cycle. I fear that they timed my kidnapping to claim Asher's heir.

My emotional tumult is soothed when he holds my hand. I know he won't let it go. The ship is moving rapidly. He and Kayden are talking in low tones. His mother is with us, along with some of her team of female warriors. I'm overwhelmed with relief and gratitude.

On Earth, if a woman had been kidnapped, no one would've saved her.

After we land in our city, Asher confers briefly with Kayden and his mother. He is still holding my hand, his touch warm and sure.

Moments later, we are walking quickly to our home with a team of guards flanking us again. When we get back to the house, I look up at the skylight where they crashed through. For now, it is closed with a thick, shimmering surface. I can still see the stars and the moon in the distance.

"How did they get here?" I ask as I turn to look at Asher.

"I should've known better," he says. "I'm sorry I didn't. I didn't think they would dare do anything like this. It's been decades since we've had this kind of breach. We had a sort of peace for over a century since the last war between our two sides. They call themselves purists. It doesn't even make sense because they're not pure. They are only alive because of the cowboys that traveled here from Earth centuries ago. They argue that since then, we must remain pure." He shakes his head. "It's ridiculous. This new leadership that has risen recently in their city is trying to return to the old ways. They don't recognize that it hurts all of us and weakens our people, preventing them from having enough mates. They took advantage of us, not recognizing the danger and thinking they wouldn't dare. We will once again put up the stronger shields and reinforce them with our new technology. We will bring this to a real fight if we must."

I'm still absorbing the reality that we're home and I'm safe. I take in what he says. "Okay," I finally say, which feels inadequate to capture the last few hours of my life.

Asher reaches for both of my hands, lifting one and turning it over before he drops a kiss in the center of my palm. His lips are warm, and his kiss like a pebble dropped into the center of a pond. Ripples of heat radiate through my body. He releases one of my hands, lifting his to smooth my hair away from my face before palming my cheek.

I stare into his eyes as a sense of peace slips through me. We're back together, and that's all that matters.

"Now that we know what they may try, you needn't worry. I'll keep you safe," he promises.

A second later, he's kissing me. I forget everything else as we tumble into the fire that snaps and crackles between us. His touch is air into the very heartbeat of our desire.

Chapter Twenty-Three

ASHER

I eye Kayden for a moment. "Jane says she thinks you met your mate when we traveled to Earth."

Kayden stands, crossing his arms. He's an imposing man, tall and broad-shouldered. A deep vein of stubbornness runs through him. He swallows as he holds my gaze. "Perhaps."

I look at my old friend and chuckle. "I mentioned to Jane this morning that you have always scoffed at the idea of the infinity pulse."

"I have," he says, his tone dry as the grasses on Earth.

"Jane said she was surprised because you seemed..." I drum my fingertips on the table before offering, "Like you had a crush."

"What the hell is a crush?" Kayden's eyes narrow with annoyance.

"That's what I asked her," I say, my lips tugging into a grin. "She said it's like when you're really into someone and really want them."

Kayden rolls his eyes. "Nadine is lovely," he declares.

"You said you never intended to mate, which, of course, devastated your father."

Kayden's father is my father's second-in-command. Like us, their bond of friendship is deep and powerful. Kayden rarely talks about it, but his mother died when he was a boy, and it devastated him and his father and his sister. He swore he would never let himself fall for anyone. He's always insisted he will be loyal to his family and to our people but that he didn't believe in the infinity pulse. His parents had it, and he's watched his father grieve for her for years.

He shrugs, spinning around to stride across my office. The windows offer a view of our city and the mountain range in the distance. The telltale silvery-blue mist shimmers above the mountains, and our sun is low in the sky.

"I never intended to mate, but I never expected to feel like this. I didn't —" He turns, his words cutting off abruptly. His gaze is troubled.

"You didn't expect how it would feel. I didn't either," I say. "There is nothing you can do about it. Not all even experience the infinity pulse. You can't stop it and won't feel it with anyone else. You know that, right?"

"Of course I know that," he says sharply. "I have other things to focus on than mating someone."

"True but, as you know, the bonding only makes you stronger."

Kayden rolls his eyes, letting out a sharp laugh. "I noticed. We need to focus on what happened with Jane and a new defense plan."

"We already have it covered. We're sending in spies. We need to know who planned it. For now, it is all in hand. You can focus on Nadine. If you'd like," I say. "Tonight, we have a dinner. Jane and I would like to invite you. I trust you'll be there?"

Kayden studies me for several quiet moments, shaking his head slowly as his lips tease with a reluctant grin. "Are you going to test me to see who else wants Nadine?"

I shrug.

"I'll be there," he mutters.

"Excellent." I stand, walking with him to the door and following him down the hallway.

"Where are you going?" he asks, glancing at me.

"Jane," I say simply.

He rolls his eyes again and keeps walking when I stop by Jane's office a few doors down and across the hallway. I've already decided we must give her a different office with an adjoining door to mine. I need her closer to me.

I rap my knuckles sharply on her door, my pulse picking up speed when I hear her voice call, "Come in!"

I step into her office and smile over at her. I lock the door behind me, and she stands from her desk, a pretty pink flush cresting on her cheeks.

"What is it?" she asks.

My cock is already swelling. She rounds her desk, coming over to meet me.

Apparently, I have a thing for desks. This desk is much nicer than that folding plastic monstrosity where I first tasted her nectar on Earth.

When she stops in front of me, I lean down to kiss her and lift her, sliding her hips onto the desk.

"You had an appointment this morning," I murmur as I nuzzle along her neck, savoring her soft, sweet sigh and the way she smells a little tart.

Her knees part easily as I step closer and drag her

hips to the edge of the desk, relieved she's wearing a skirt.

"I did," she says when I finally lift my head and look into her eyes.

"Well?"

"I'm pregnant," she says, a smile unfurling across her face.

Satisfaction surges through me. I move a little closer and rock my hips into the cradle of hers. "Of course, you are," I murmur. "I knew it."

She takes a quick breath. I can't help myself. I reach out to find her bare, wet pussy and tease my fingers into it.

"Asher," she whispers.

"I love you," I whisper in return.

Chapter Twenty-Four

JANE

I run my hand over my round belly. I feel, well, just round all over. My breasts are swollen and sore to the touch, and my belly is so big. I'm due any day now.

Back when I lived on Earth, I remember women worrying about having babies because there was only one doctor for the whole town. Here, we have an entire medical facility and a hospital with more advanced technology. More than that, I don't fear someone ignoring my pain and treating me as if I exist solely to have a baby. Oh, don't get me wrong, I completely understand that giving birth to the heir of the royal family is important. But being somewhere where women are loved and savored is incredible.

I walk from our bedroom out to the kitchen, where Asher is getting juice for me. He turns, his eyes meeting mine from across the room. Even now when I feel frumpy and round, there's heat in his gaze.

"How are you feeling this morning?" He sets the glass of juice down on the counter and turns to face me as I approach.

He stops in front of me, leaning down to dust a

kiss on my neck. Goose bumps rise on my skin because I'm enthralled to my husband.

"Ready to pop," I tease when he lifts his head.

He slides his palm over my belly, his touch soothing and protective. "The doctor said any day now," he murmurs.

Just then, I feel an intense sensation, and wetness spills between my thighs. "I think my water broke!" I burst out.

What follows is a blur. Asher rushes me to the medical facility. Blessedly, the birth lasts less than six hours. Asher is with me through all of it. When it's finally over and I hear the healthy cry of our baby, I roll my head to the side and meet Asher's gaze. He squeezes my hand.

"It's a boy," the doctor announces.

Moments later, they lay my baby boy on my chest, and I hold him close, my eyes landing on his tiny tail. I smile at Asher.

That night, we're resting in bed. Asher has basically been my servant since we got home from the medical facility. A nurse had come with us and made sure everything was set up for us and the baby.

I'm still exhausted from the birth. I look over at Asher as he rolls to his side, his hand smoothing my hair away from my forehead. "My princess," he murmurs as he presses a kiss on my cheek. "Rest now."

I fall into a sleep.

———

It's been a full two months, and my body has been recovering from giving birth. Our baby is healthy at home and growing so fast that I can't even believe it.

Our baby boy is named after Asher, and we call him Ash.

Meanwhile, my doctor has just told me that I'm cleared for full activity again. I never, *never* could've imagined being so desperate to be with a man again that I almost ignored my doctor's orders. But now, I'm clear.

I hurry into our home, where Asher is standing in the kitchen. His eyes lock with mine. Before I can ask, he says, "Ash just went down for a nap."

I practically skip across the room, stopping in front of him. "We're clear," I murmur.

He reaches for me, pulling me close. I feel the swollen length of his arousal pressing against my belly. "Oh, thank you," he murmurs.

In a fiery second, we're kissing and tearing at each other's clothes. Asher looks at me, lifting me onto the counter. We still have a thing for desks and counters.

My breasts are aching, and I cry out when he teases my nipples with his mouth. My pussy pulses with every beat of my heart.

"Please," I rasp.

He draws away. "I need you," he growls.

I see his cock, swollen and proud, with cum rolling down the length as he steps closer.

"You have me," I whisper as his fingers tease around my slippery, swollen clit.

Asher

Chapter Twenty-Five

ASHER

I have missed being buried inside Jane. So *very* much. Yet the wait makes it all the more meaningful. Jane, my princess, has given me everything I wanted. She is mine, and I am hers. And now, we have our own small family.

I look down at her pussy, swollen and slippery with the juices of her arousal. Her clit is poking out, so needy. My balls draw tight.

I lift my eyes to hers again, sliding a hand around the sweet curve of her hip as I draw her closer to the edge of the counter. Her legs dangle as I fist my cock, smearing the crown through her folds as my seed spurts out a little.

"Asher! Please!" she gasps.

I give her just what she needs, sheathing myself in her slick, rippling core.

She's coming only moments later as I pump into her. Mine follows swiftly once she's crying out and clenching hard around my cock.

While Jane's given me all I want, more than anything, I just want her, us. Because together, we are home. I hold her against me hours later as we fall asleep.

Hours later, she's fully dressed, in the kitchen, and holding our baby. I look over at them from across the room, feeling full and complete. They are my everything.

Weeks later, we have an event to christen Ash. I let my gaze scan the crowd. We're still dealing with the threats from the other city, but things are good here for us.

I hold Jane's hand. She smiles up at me, her chin lifting high. I love her thread of pride. I'm always grateful she was brave enough to come here and start all over.

Once our son is christened, we stand together, and my parents smile at us indulgently. I reach for Jane's hand, lifting her knuckles to brush a kiss across them. "My princess."

EPILOGUE

Nadine

"Come in," I say when I hear the knock on my door.

I live in a tiny apartment. Really tiny. It's all I could afford after I finally scraped up to the nerve to leave my abusive boyfriend. He's rich, and he lives in the green zone. He told me he wouldn't even help me, and I don't care. This one-room apartment is a breath of fresh air compared to my life with him.

I have a shitty job and live in a tiny apartment, and I've never felt more free in my life. There's just that forever anxiety prickling down my spine that he's going to come back.

I open the door, and a sense of panic claws around my throat. I stare at him. "What are you doing here, Chad?"

My ex, who, objectively speaking, is handsome, narrows his eyes. "I thought you would come to your senses a little sooner," he says, brushing past me as he strides into my apartment.

He looks around the one room with a sneer. It might be small, but it's cute. I have my own phone for the first time ever since I met him. Life on Earth may be hellish, but we still have technology. That's something.

I have a shelf on the wall where I keep my clothes folded. I'm standing in front of it beside the door. He moves so fast, I'm not prepared. He shoves me against the shelf, and I feel the square metal edge dig in a line against my back. My breath is knocked out of my lungs for a moment.

I keep my wits, and I kick him in the balls hard. "Fuck you! Get the hell out of here."

He's groaning on the floor. I step around him, my pulse thundering through my body as panic and fear give me an unexpected surge of strength. I swing the door open and shove him out on the dirt.

I grab my purse, relieved I already have my phone and keys tucked into it. Racing through the door, I step around him and walk away quickly. I don't even feel the slightest twinge of guilt.

I'm so tired of Chad and his family. At this point, I'll hide if I have to. As I walk down the sidewalk with the sand blowing around me, my eyes land on a little flyer about moving to a new planet. I don't hesitate and simply walk to the address listed. I have less than nothing to lose.

When I see the line gathered outside the office building, I pause and glance around. Aside from showing up for work and trying not to bake in the boiling hot sun, there aren't many crowds. Not these days.

I hesitate before I see the sign posted. *Princess Jane invites you to Aphroditea. Let's face it, life is hell on Earth these days if you're a woman. Come join us on a new planet. We need women. Bonus: women are revered here. Hop in line, and you'll find out all about it.*

I have zero reasons not to get in line. I join the

line, fidgeting with my purse strap and wondering if anyone will care that I have a black eye.

There are quiet murmurs, wondering if Princess Jane is some kind of joke. Although, if you read our news online and in the old magazines we occasionally find, there's tons of news about royalty on Earth.

It's not all sturm and drang here on Earth. We have a lively world on our Internet, which somehow runs even though power is scarce. It's generated from the green zone.

Eventually, I make it inside the building. I'm interviewed by the alleged Princess Jane herself. She even has a name tag that says it.

Jane runs through an explanation, sharing that Aphroditea has had humans on it for centuries. Apparently, cowboys from back in the day from both the United States and France traveled there. They even have creatures similar to horses. "I know it sounds wild," she adds with a smile. "They have mated for centuries, like other planets."

"Except Earth," I offer dryly. "Because we're dumbasses, and we were busy destroying our own planet."

Jane rolls her eyes. "So true."

"So why do they need women there?" I ask.

"There's an annual festival to honor women there. Two years ago, a storm struck the area during the festival and many women died."

"Are the men human?"

"There are some human men there, but those that have descended from the space cowboys—"

"Are they really space cowboys?" I prompt with a sly grin. I like Jane and actually feel comfortable cracking a joke.

Jane flushes as she smiles. "Yes, they are. They are human-like but not entirely human," she explains.

"Since they've mated for years with humans, we are very similar. Their skin is more bronze. Some of them have tails, but not all of them. I'll be honest, though, the tails are sexy," she says with an enthusiastic nod.

Jane seems familiar to me, and I can't place why. I'm pretty sure I've seen her before. When she's finished explaining this whole, honestly, wild situation, I say, "You seem familiar to me. Do I know you?"

She shrugs. "I'm not sure. I've only been away from Earth for a few weeks. I saw the ad online for a princess. I was tipsy when I was reading it, so I applied." She pauses, her eyes going wide. "Now, I'm actually a princess there."

"No joke?" I press, almost dumbfounded.

"No joke. Trust me, I thought it had to be a joke too."

"Where did you work when you were here?"

"At one of the offices in the main factory."

We have three factories in town, the main one being the largest. We make products for the green zone. I work in one of the smaller ones.

"Wait a second," I say. "Were you engaged to Kyle Smith?"

Jane lets out a sigh. "I sure was. My not-so-best friend screwed around with him. Because she really wanted to go to the green zone." Her lips twist. "I thought I was going to get to go. Even though that whole thing sucked, I'm glad it happened. If I hadn't caught them, I never would've applied to leave the planet. Trust me, life is so much better on Aphroditea. Do you have family or anything? Because that's an issue. We don't want anyone leaving family or children behind."

I shake my head, my heart twisting. "Nope. My

parents died. It's just me. And my ex-boyfriend beats me."

Jane's eyes narrow. "Well, then, I think you're perfect for this."

"When does this happen?" I ask, experiencing a surge of relief followed by anxiety.

"Today. Do you need anything from your apartment?"

I shake my head quickly. "Nothing at all. I can leave from here." Relief washes through me, and tears sting my eyes.

Jane reaches out and clasps one of my hands in hers. Her grounding touch is comforting. "I promise. This will be a better life."

Just then, I feel the hairs rise on the back of my neck, and a prickle of awareness sizzles up my spine. I'm instantly drawn to look toward a door opening on the side of this large conference room. There are several tables, and other women are being interviewed. A tall and imposing man enters.

I know instantly that he's not from here. His eyes narrow as his head whips around, his gaze locking with mine from across the room.

It literally feels as if a flame leaps through the air between us, leaving a wake of sparks across the room.

My pulse pounds, and my breath becomes short. I've never felt anything like this.

Flustered and unsettled, I glance back toward Jane. "Who is that?"

Her eyes are warm. "That's Kayden. He's second-in-command to Prince Asher. There's this thing—" She pauses, considering her words. "Their people believe in a true mate, but they don't each find one. When I met Asher, it was the most intense thing I've ever experienced. Maybe Kayden is your mate."

While I'm trying to absorb that crazy idea, the man in question walks straight over to me. His bronzed skin almost shimmers. He looks at Jane and nods. "Your Princess."

I almost burst out laughing at that. Kayden's golden eyes hold mine, and I cannot look away. He studies me before reaching for my hand. "Follow me," he says.

I'm pretty sure I'd walk through fire for this man. I put my hand in his and stand. "Can I go with him?" I belatedly look back at Jane.

She smiles, waving us away. "Please go." She glances at Kayden. "Be nice."

————

Jane, or Princess Jane I should say, has invited all of us over for dinner. I'm still a little shocked at my situation. In a matter of one single day, my life has changed forever. Everything went to hell before I saw that ad, and I'm still trying to recover.

Aside from being hot as hell, Earth has been my personal hell lately.

I'd had an epically bad day. Then I saw the ad when I was walking to the store. I just walked right on over and never went home. I don't care where my asshole of an ex is.

Beyond being the aforementioned asshole, he also occasionally gave me a black eye. I thought we were done for good, but his family wouldn't let me go. They had money and power, and I had nothing and no one. I'm a fighter, though, which my mom told me was a problem when I was younger.

"Fuck that shit," I mutter to myself, shaking the

bad memories away. I'm not even on Earth anymore. I can forget about all of it.

I slip out of my bedroom into the bathroom and take a quick look at myself. Fortunately, the bruising on my back shouldn't be that bad. The bruise under my eye is still there.

Jane has even made sure we all had clothes. I slip out of the soft T-shirt I slept in and select a flowing dress. I glance toward the mirror, twisting to look over my shoulders. There's a line of a bruise down one side. I hope it doesn't matter.

When I arrive at the dinner, which is being hosted at Jane's beautiful home, I'm beyond nervous. There are men everywhere and most of them aren't human, although they look close to it. Except for the tails and shimmery skin.

As I watch Princess Jane with Prince Asher, it's hard to believe she lived on Earth mere weeks ago. The prince appears enthralled to her. I can't help but hope and pray I mate with a man who treats me with the kindness he gives her.

I'm sitting at the table when I feel heat shimmer over my skin. I know without even looking that Kayden is near me. I can't help but look. It's as if an invisible force connects us. He's approaching from the side. The second our eyes lock, my belly swoops and my breath seizes in my lungs.

He stops beside me, his golden eyes sweeping over me. He holds his hand out. "Come with me."

Thank you for reading Asher & Jane's story - I hope you loved it!

. . .

Up next in the Match Made in Space Series is Bride for the Space Cowboy. A grumpy alien cowboy in need of a bride, a human woman on the run looking to escape, and an intergalactic matchmaking service. Buckle up for more space cowboy spice!

One-click to pre-order: Bride for the Space Cowboy - due out November 2024

Sign up for my newsletter, so you can receive information about upcoming new releases & deals: https://phoebebelle.com/

ABOUT THE AUTHOR

Phoebe Belle lives on Earth. She loves escaping into happily-ever-afters, her family - human, canine and maybe even alien (not willing to rule that out because you never know!) - coffee and cooking.

http://phoebebelle.com/

facebook.com/phoebebellegalaxyromance
instagram.com/phoebebellegalaxyromance